Tales from the Mike-Side

Tales from the Mike-Side

Deranged

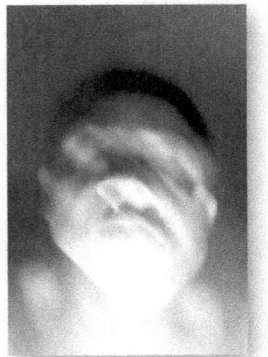

The Soul Catcher
Maybe I Died

Michael Kent

ISBN: 0998999016
ISBN 13: 9780998999012

DERANGED: FORWARD

You are about to read the first-hand account of one man's descent into depravity. Like a moth near a flame, he flirted with schizophrenia…on purpose. While experimenting on his own brain, he meddled in the inner workings of his mind. His brain had no choice but to defend itself from his very own consciousness.

Derived from the personal journal of a man who lost his way, this book is not for the squeamish or faint of heart. These are no vague recollections, but rather the immediate ravings from the mind of a maniac.

Do not attempt to recreate these experiments at home. You may incur permanent brain damage. The subject admits that he should have been under medical and psychiatric supervision.

You've been warned. Turn the page at your own risk.

DERANGED: PROLOG

"**S**hut up and sit back down!"

"Okay, okay - wait. Gimme a minute. I was just... You guys just dragged me in here."

"Nobody dragged you in here. I don't have all night, Walter. So, what's it gonna be. You came in here, *voluntarily*, to talk. So, talk."

Oh God - he's right. This is my reality. I'm Walter Michael Harris. I must have passed out. Shake it off.

"Look - I can't do this. Those guys are maniacs."

"Where you gonna go, Walter. Go ahead - there's the door."

I was scared. Not of prison. I know how to handle myself. And I grew up around killers; hard people with cold hearts. They come at you crazy; you come back crazier. If they don't back down, you rip out their throat.

I was more afraid of who I'd become. I grew up a softy. But I came around over the years. It started with little things. Like looking the other way when someone got stabbed. As opposed to not being there in the first place.

You're dead either way. You might as well tell em.

"Okay detective. Strap in. And I'll tell you what we did last night. I'll tell you; but I won't name names. I just need to get this one off my chest. And who else am I gonna tell.

We caught a guy wearing a wire. We both know who the guy is…I mean, was."

"Who is we?" That stupid cop asked, as if this was my first interrogation. I just ignored him.

"We found one of your wireless bugs, in his pocket, with some *real* quarters. You guys are stupid. You gotta switch it up sometimes."

That's when detective dumbass kicked over a chair. I looked right through him; right to where his head connected to the top of his spine. And he knew not to come around that table. Another, heavy-set detective came in from behind the two-way mirror to calm things down. But I already had things under control.

"Are you listening, detective Peete?"

Then Peete sent the heavy-set guy out of the room.

"We snatched your guy out the back way; right under your noses, and drove him to his own meat market. You know those metal tables they use to cut through sides of beef? The ones with a band-saw at one end?"

Peete nodded, snapped his finger twice, and pointed to the window. I knew he was telling the guys behind the glass to get the right people listening.

"Yeah. I know the ones."

"Well I'd never seen a table like that before last night. And it turned my stomach when they slammed him down on it. You know why?"

Peete's lip twitched on one side.

"I don't know, Walter. Why don't you tell me?"

"Gimme a cigarette."

Peete slid me the pack, and a lighter.

"Ahhh…the menthol. They turned on the saw, while he laid there begging for his life. But here's the kicker."

And I knew it would get a rise out of Pistol Peete. That's what we called him, because he shot two innocent bystanders in a running gun battle.

"They never laid a finger on him. They just dared him to move. And he didn't. Then they flipped the switch that started the table moving."

I took another pull and blew smoke rings. I waited for them to hit Peete in the face.

"Your snitch would rather die on that table, than be tortured by those psychos."

"What psychos?"

"Come on, Peete; stop interrupting. So the guy lays there grimacing, while the table pushes him head first into that band-saw. I thought for sure he'd jump off the table; we all did. But he just twitched a little…until the blade disappeared in the top of his head."

I knew what was coming. Peete tossed his cookies, right there on the table. I yelled the rest, to keep his attention.

"The guy was laying in the fetal position. So next it cut through his arms. They turned it off, after it cut his legs off."

Peete shook his head and ran out. He couldn't take no more. The heavy-set cop came in and tried to calm me down, with a backhand across my jaw. I just spat blood in his face and kept going.

"You know what happened then? They chopped through his neck with a meat cleaver. None of us wanted to touch what was left. Blood ran off the table like a warm slurpy."

I laughed for extra effect. I wanted to terrorize everybody in the police station - the whole building. So now, here comes a shrink with a needle. And I'm still yelling while they piled on top of me.

"And then two of those sick bastards put his head back together, and wrapped it up in meat paper. They taped it closed, like it was a pot roast. They made me put it out in the store front for some square to take home for dinner."

It took six of them to take me down; six cops, a can of pepper spray, and a shot.

"Go see for yourselves. It's right there in that assholes meat market, on the corner of Sixth and Main."

That was the last thing I remember, before waking up in that moldy cell. They must have put me under the jail.

There is a place in my mind that I call home. I don't know why my mind chose *that* place to call home; I only lived there for two years.

A modest two-story brick house with three bedrooms and a basement, seems to be at the core of my soul. And I go back there often, to work out the battles taking place in my subconsciousness; those things that lie beneath the here and the now.

That corner lot with a detached garage, in a well-manicured, green neighborhood, stopped being a house in the material world long, long ago. It now exists as a construct in my dreams. Though the physical house still stands, I haven't been inside it in years. It was my mom's house. She died too young; quite some time ago.

I left my childhood in that house. And I left sin there. But I still wake up *there*, when I go to sleep *here*. And I'm fifty something years old, in my childhood bedroom, at my mother's house.

"Wake up you deadbeat, it's four in the afternoon."

"Oh, hey mom. You're home early. I was just taking a nap."

"You been here more than a year, Mark. I'm sick of you. Why don't you just go and live with one of your kids?"

My dream mama doesn't know that I don't want to be here anymore than she wants me here. I used to have a life. I used to be somebody. If I had my wife's phone number, I could call her. Maybe she'd take me back. When was the last time I sent her money for the house note? Too long.

"I see you rented my sister's room out again."
    "She's not a deadbeat like you. She's got her own place now."
    "Whatever, mom. Can you tell those kids to stay out of my room?"
    If I had gas money, I could drive back to California. If I had gas money.

I'm not a doctor; not of any sort. I don't have a degree in physiology or kinesiology. But I do have a body. And there are things that I learned about my body without being taught.

I learned that if I could balance on two feet, and put one foot in front of the other, without falling, I could get places without crawling on all fours. I'm pretty sure I would've learned to walk, even if I'd never seen anyone else do it.

I learned to make sounds with my throat and tongue. And if I got the sounds just right, I could move big people into action. So I listened intently to the sounds that people made. And I learned to associate sounds with meanings.

I found out that some sounds related to *things*, and that other sounds related to *actions*. It took a while, but I eventually figured out that some words - like *hot*, *bad*, and *no*, had negative connotations. And that *good* and *yes* had positive connotations.

I learned to look *on*, *under*, or *next to* - to find things that others knew the location of. So, by age two, I understood the difference between nouns, verbs, adjectives and prepositions. All, without even knowing my ABC's.

I learned how to ride a bike, without being a physicist. And how to swim, without understanding hydrodynamics. I could stand on my head, jump and play, without any coaxing whatsoever.

I have a body. I learned to use it, because I have unlimited access to it. I learned karate, and how to fly a plane, without killing myself in the process. It's my body, and I can practice using it as much, or as little, as I want.

Why wouldn't I be able to experiment with the only brain that I have unlimited access to? This brain is *my* brain. I can come to understand what it is capable of, without being a brain surgeon or psychiatrist. We know that our brains are capable of learning things outside of our skulls; like math, or the way to the bank.

I know, by trying, that my head turns only so far in either direction. I can run, only so fast, and jump only so high. I know I can't fly without a plane, because I've tried. Haven't you?

There are things about our brains that we never even tried to understand. Maybe because we can't see them, or because they have no moving parts. But our brains just might be the most fantastic structures in the entire known universe. Yet many of us know more about cosmic black holes than we do about the universe that lies between our ears, and have direct access to – always.

Of all the different types of doctors that deal in the science of the brain, none of them use their own brain as the brain under study. Because their studies are external, their access is limited. And their feedback, more limited still. By using my own brain as the object of study, not only do I have unlimited access, I also have unlimited feedback.

When I was fifteen, there was a pretty little girl that lived in the corner house; diagonally, across from mom's, on the other side of the intersection. I never spoke to her. I was too shy. That house got torn down, somewhere in dream world time. Two homes were built in its place. One facing south, and the other facing east. I can see both of them from the upstairs bathroom window at my mother's house.

The house facing south mirrors mom's, which faces north. A respectable family lives there. Which is surprising because the eastern facing house is a 'dope' house. They sell heroin, right out of the front door. I can always tell when they're open for business. There's a line of junkies under the overhang of the small porch, or people are going onto the porch hopeful, and leaving ecstatic.

I know because I was a heroin addict at aged fifteen, and eighteen, and at twenty-one. And at every other time I visited mom's house after I moved out - until I got sober, when I was thirty. Now, at fifty-something (in dream land), I'm a junkie again. And there's the dope house right outside mom's front door. I don't think the dealer knows me that well. But only because I'm broke most of the time.

But I have money today, so what'll it be? Gas to get back to California? Or will I binge on heroin until I run out of money? Then I'd be stuck here with mom for another month. Maybe I should find my wife's phone number and send her some money. Then I'd actually have a place to go when I got to California.

But I can't do all three. And doing only two, doesn't make sense. I could send my wife money to pay the house note, and not have gas to drive across eight states. I could hop in my old car, hope it doesn't break down, and end up homeless when I got there. I could do one of those, and get a 'fix' - which makes no sense.

Or I could scoot across the street, right quick, before they run out. Just like I've done every month. When was the last time I sent money to my wife? Too long. She's probably moved on.

Last night I went too far. I entered a place that I've been getting thrown out of for years. A place that I always associated with my former career as an aerospace engineer. A mistake easily made since both places have lots of office space, for meetings, and lots of factory space where highly technical operations are being performed.

At my old job the product was space satellites, for the most part. But research and development for new technologies was commonplace. The dreamscape and the real-world workplace are both the size of college campuses. I find myself in the dreamscape facsimile, on a nightly basis. More often than I dream of my mother's house.

At my mother's dream house, though not welcome, I am tolerated. At my job dreamscape, the authorities are trying to arrest me. Their message is clear. I'm not supposed to be there.

Getting in is easy. I'm never challenged. Getting out is the problem. I've been there so often that there are undercover agents at every exit - from the office buildings and the sterile factory areas. And from the, not so sterile, factory areas and raw material storage yards.

I go there to help out…every night. I don't get paid, but I wish I did. I'm on disability for major depression, in real life. I always thought those dreams meant that I missed being a rocket scientist. There used to be one man there who could spot me as an outsider. He told me, on more than one occasion, that if he saw me in one of those buildings again, he'd have me arrested. This, after marching me to the exit himself a few times.

I only go there to help out because I miss the high-tech challenge. I'd go there to sit in on meetings, from time to time, just so I would know what they were up to. And then one day, one of the men running a meeting gave me an action to complete. So, I had a task, for which I had to report my progress. And then my name started flying around, as part of the organization. But the spoiler that recognized me was around often enough to keep me sneaking.

Either the man retired *from my brain*, or I am too involved for him to police me on his own. Eventually they put my picture at the exit gates. But I knew which exits were guarded. That was a few years ago. These days, I am public enemy number one.

I learned to dodge them. They can only detain me on company property. If I made it to a public street, I was safe. They caught me a few times, but they couldn't hold me. Most times I'd just fly over the fence between the guard posts.

But last night, I went too far with my brain experiments. I finally questioned the people working in one of the big factory areas. I wasn't ready for the answers.
"Does this factory represent my brain?"
A young woman answered:
"No, silly. This is just the reception area."
So, I asked a group of young men:
"If this place represents the reception area, how big he is my brain?"
One of them smiled and said:
"The size of a city."
I found I could control the reception area with my words. I could say *green*, and the laminated factory floor would change from standard gray to green. I could change the characters from male to female, Black to White, brunette to blonde, and so forth. So, I asked:

"Are you saying that I have a, city-sized, brain under my control?"
The young man told me:
"There are parts of it that control you."

I've been at this self-brain analysis for decades. I just didn't know I was doing it. Over the years, I've gained both insight and talent. It took forever to learn to fly. I still have difficulty from time to time. Pick up enough speed and I can crash through an entire office building, feeling every brick wall and drywall, and out the other side. Flying is almost a necessity and self-brain experimentation. I'll stop here to explain one of the foundational theories that I've formulated.

The brain is a, geographically allocated, super processor. There is, within that geography, the place we experience as the *here and now*. The *here and now* is the conscious mind that we use to navigate our daily lives.

Neurons fire in a billion networks of interconnecting synapses, at an average of twenty times per second, during our waking hours. When the synapses use up their chemical fuel of sugar and amino acids, we become mentally fatigued and in need of sleep. Those sugar and amino acid fuels are known as neural transmitters.

While my neurons rest from a million and a half electrical firings, the synapses' chemical storehouses that enable neighboring neurons to fire, are replenished. While the geographic location of my *here and now* recuperates, my consciousness (still active) drifts to another physical location in my brain. My consciousness often moves to locations that used to be in the *here and now*.

Consciousness is a collection of neurological networks. I read that we are blessed with a hundred billion neurons, at brain maturity - around fifteen years old. Each of those hundred billion neurons are connected, through synapses, to ten thousand other neurons. That's one *quadrillion* connections. Maybe that's why teenagers (think they) know everything.

I believe that our consciousness, or *here and now* awareness forms in the womb, taking up as much brain real estate as it takes to be a fetus. Birth presents a quantum leap of new information to process, and new born baby problems to solve: nursing, crying, and finding comfort outside of mother's womb.

In response, the *here and now* processing must move into fresh territory, where new born baby neurological networks can form. You see, I don't believe the brain normally overwrites its historical neurological networks, because it might need them again in an emergency. For example, taking on the fetal position in times of tumultuous emotional stress. Or the fight-or-flight networks, which we must snap to, in times of immediate danger.

In my mother's house, I am in my late fifties. My mother died when I was forty, but my little sister still lives there. The house and the neighborhood look like they did when I lived there at fifteen.

It's the holidays, with relatives coming and going, the way they did when mom was alive. My cousins drop by to visit without calling ahead. Nobody made appointments to visit back then. We just showed up, and were glad to see each other. Sometimes they stayed for ten minutes, other times they stayed for days.

Then mom came downstairs and started fiddling with pots and pans. Nobody said anything. They just assumed she was going to fix us some-thing to eat. It happens this way a lot. And I always wonder why no one ever says anything.

"Y'all do know she's dead - right?"

Somehow I get a ticket to the *here and now*, and wake up in my little square house, with my wife of one year.

I love my life in the *here and now*. My house is filled with love, sweet smells and the beauty that only a woman can bring. I'm fine with a brown couch, a bed, four place settings and a big-screen TV.

My consciousness rarely sleeps. It just goes somewhere else when the *here and now* neural network needs to rest and recharge.

I'm retired. My wife works out of town, so she's gone fourteen hours a day. My kids, and hers, are all grown and gone. So, I have plenty of opportunities to do dream research. That's what I call napping. Don't get me wrong. I enjoy a good nap, but my dream life is more than fantastic. And I'm testing the limits of accessibility and control.

It's getting a little scary. I finally told my wife how far I had gone. She wants me to stop. I probably should stop. My brain has been trying to protect itself against my meddling.

Have you ever heard of 'lucid' dreaming? How can I describe it? It's probably easier than describing colors to a person that's been blind from birth. *That's* hard to even imagine, if you can see. But I'll give it a try.

Think back to one of your days on the beach. The smell of brine is in the air and you feel salt spray on your face. Think about the gentle breeze stroking the hair on your arms. The sun is shining on your face, but not on your back. Maybe you picked up a handful of sand, and let it run between your fingers.

A lucid dream is not like remembering the beach, at all. It's not like imagining the beach. A lucid dream is like *being* at the beach. In a lucid dream, you are conscious. You may be aware that you are dreaming. Once you know you're dreaming, you marvel at the reality of it all. Feel the sand slipping through your fingers on the beaches of your mind. Feel your feet, in water up to your ankles.

Fly off to a rural dreamscape. Sense the crack of a lightning bolt striking the branch of a nearby tree. You see it, and hear it. You feel it in your gut and smell ozone in the air. Listen as the branch cracks and takes out a powerline, that dances electric - way too close to your feet.

Lucid dreams are alive with color and textures. Watch sunlight reflect from each of a thousand windshields on a distant freeway. Every detail is perfect. But you know you're dreaming. Why not hold onto the experience? Why not explore? Go ahead, pick up that turtle. Feel it move in your hands. Lucid dreams are interactive realities, put together by a brain that puts together the reality of the *here and now*.

Our brains make sense of a continuous input of visual images. It figures out perspective and distance, and relative speeds and directions of individual objects. Crossing a busy street, on foot, presents an almost infinite number of visual variables; many of which would cause death if we misperceived them.

While watching a live football game, our brains make sense of a half billion pixels that change by the millisecond. Imagine being a player on the field, dodging tackles that would maim most of us. We drive cars and play catch with our children. Some of us even perform brain surgery without scrambling the patient's brain.

Our brains process five senses, in real time, to construct what is known to us as reality. And our brains are good at it. Better and more reliable than any supercomputer. All of this without any help whatsoever from us. Given a set of sensory inputs, our brains create a reality in which we may exist and explore. And it doesn't care where the inputs come from. They can be *live*; through our eyes, ears, nose, mouth and skin. Or they can come from memory. It makes no difference.

All our senses feed into their own unique storage areas, inside our brains. Tactile memory is stored in our parietal lobes. That's why you know how heavy an object will be, before you pick it up. Get it wrong and you'll pull your shoulder out of socket, or throw that hot coffee right in your face.

Like tactile memory, visual memories are stored in the area in which they are processed - the occipital (visual) cortex. Smells are stored in the limbic system, with enough precision to pick out the individual ingredients in a casserole or apple pie. Hearing is processed and stored in the temporal lobes.

Again, I'm no doctor. The point that I am making is that when memories are played back from the areas in which they are processed, it is the same as if they came from the organ that sensed them. I can't quite taste in my dreams. Not yet anyway. But almost. I'll have to work on that one.

I believe in my case, that lucid dreaming came as a side effect to my antidepressant. But, over time I learned to cultivate and encourage lucidity. I've had lots of practice; thousands of hours. I'm *really* good at it. Consider me a black belt.

Our brains record every sensory input that it receives. And that - for all five senses. Think about it. How many faces can you recognize? Certainly more than a hundred or a thousand. Maybe ten thousand? How many people have you actually looked at in your life? A better question might be, how many have you noticed.

Unless you're a politician, the number is probably smaller than you think. How many times have you heard someone say:

"I never forget a face?"

I was just browsing my Facebook friends, as I often do during my down time between experiments. I don't know who posted a picture of the girl of three or four, sitting in her pint-sized chair. But the picture triggered a nearly sixty-year-old memory, when my stepfather brought home a little chair especially for me.

"Look what your dad got you," my mother said with emphasis on the word dad.

Somehow, I remember that he painted the chair himself. I remember the texture of the fresh blue paint as I write. And now that I'm tugging on the thread of that memory, I remember the smell of the fresh paint.

Our brain wastes no memories. It may need them one day to save its own existence, or to make a point for an author. We subconsciously remember every clock; the sound of its chimes, and the temperature in the room in which we saw it. We remember songs that we don't even realize we heard. We remember the touch of love. What a gift our memories are.

Here's the point I'm getting at. Our dreams are made of *fetched* memories. Each dream is put together from pieces of stored memories. A car from the visual cortex. The sound of an engine from the temporal cortex. The resistance in the gas pedal, from tactile memory. And all of them, not necessarily from the same car. I know this not from external research, but from experimenting on my own sleeping brain.

In my dreamscape, I saw a clock on the wall. A unique and specific clock, containing complete visual detail. I, inadvertently, looked away (you can do that in the dream). When I looked back, it was a different clock. No way, I thought. So, I looked away and back again. Sure enough, there was a different clock in the last one's place. Again and again, I experimented with that clock. It would seem the new clock was retrieved from visual memory, every time I asked the dreamscape for a clock.

I had discovered the nature of the construct of dreams. I *fetched* that clock ten times or so. Each time a different clock was *fetched*. Until there was a mistake in the *fetch* routine, and it came back with something other than a clock. I don't remember what came back with that particular *fetch* mistake. But for example, if it came back with a book instead of a clock, a different book came back with every subsequent *fetch*.

I learned over real-time years of experimentation, that if I liked an image I saw, I should refrain from looking away. Think about the ramifications. A beautiful woman - *fetch* - a different beautiful woman - *fetch* - a not so beautiful woman - *fetch*... *fetch* - oops. Squid tentacles instead of legs - *fetch* - squid.

However, some constructs remain intact, in pseudo-reality for the entirety of the dream sequence. My absolute most lovely and pleasant constructs are my children. I only know I'm dreaming because they are younger than they are in real life.

Oh God, I saw my twenty-year-old son as a fifteen-year-old. I hugged him and held on tight. I felt the strength in his back and kissed him on the side of his freshly cut hair. I told him about it in the *here and now*, and he thanked me for the hug.

I recently saw my twenty-six-year-old daughter at eighteen. She knew absolutely everything. Just like she does now.

"Can I stay a while?"

She allowed it. Just being in the same room with her, watching her pack for a trip, meant the world to me. And so, I play with my children, when they were kids, every time I get a chance.

Are you interested in lucid dreams yet? Can you imagine the attraction - the temptation, the desire to control. I have learned to hold lucid constructs intact, because lucidity is a conscious state. Awake and aware I study and enjoy the construct that lies behind my closed eyes. I am here and there, at the same time.

Maybe I should stop before the two become one.

Now, call on the thunder. For beyond lucid dream recognition, lies lucid dream exploration. And beyond exploration, lies lucid dream control. Go ahead - venture too far. Play God in your own head. I was amazed the first time I stumbled into the realm of lucid dream control.

One sunny day, while standing in one of the many parking lots on the campus where I worked for twenty-four years, I called in the storm. Much like faith, in the Bible, the lucid dreamscape is pliable by our words.

"Storm," I commanded.

And the clouds accumulated like a movie, in fast motion. Then the rain poured, wetting my face and clothes. And then came thunder that shook my bones. Forks of lightning split the dark and stormy sky. Again, I thought *no way*. So I spoke the words:

"Blue sky."

And the storm dispersed, with the natural process of a passing storm.

"Storm - blue sky - storm - blue sky."

My brain complied by *fetching* the elements of weather as I commanded.

Dare I, try it with the people in my dreams? In my dreamscapes, everybody knows me. I used to be well known and highly regarded. I found myself walking with a group of my peers while they picked my brains for the secrets to success. Yes... I'll experiment on them.

"You - stop."

And that one would stop.

"You - talk."

And that one would talk.

"Stop - go - left - right."

I stopped short of telling one to bark like a dog. It doesn't really matter because they are just animated *fetches*. They are not real - are they?

At some point, I began teasing the ones that wanted to do things *their* way. A dream cop pulled me over.

"License and registration please?"

"Come on man, you are not even real."

I laughed, but *he* didn't know he wasn't real.

"Step out of the car please."

"Dude, you're just a figment in my dream. Do I have to prove it to you?"

And I loved showing him. And all others that challenged or disagreed with me. After all, it's just a lucid dream.

"I'll just open my eyes and you'll be gone."

"Sure you will sir. You'll just open your eyes…".

Why did I get such satisfaction from opening my eyes, and watching him fade from the *here and now*? But you know what? He was a *there* for a few seconds. They always are. Right there in reality, in my bedroom where I woke up. And they seem to be troubled that they are fading away. I don't do it all the time, because it always works…every time. For now, anyway.

Most of the time, while I know I'm dreaming, I have no idea where I was when I went to sleep. I'm lost in dreamland, not knowing where my prone body lies. I could wake up on vacation in Hawaii, on one of my couches, or in prison - if I wake up at all. I'm always glad when I wake up in my bed with my wife, in our little square house on the hill.

W hat is thought, other than an opinion about our surroundings? Short of thinking, we just stare off into space, without judgment. In past *here and now's*, I'd drive for hours with my two youngest sons. There was always chatter when the three of us were together. One day I realized that there wasn't much talking going on when the littlest one wasn't there. He never shut up, so peace and quiet was welcomed.

One day there was just me and my quiet son. And I asked him:
"What are you thinking about?"
His answer surprised me. I was quite concerned when he answered:
"Nothing."
"How can you be *not* thinking of anything?"
"I don't know, I'm just not."
"Do you see the mountains and the trees?'
"Yes."
"Well, aren't you thinking something about them?"
"No."
I pressed him.
"It's impossible not to think of anything."
He laughed and said:
"Maybe for you."
It became an inside joke that he was the only person, his little brother and I knew, that could live in the *here and now* without thinking. We didn't put it like that but that's what we meant.

I happened to be staring out of a public window today. A lady came into view pushing a baby stroller. At the exact same time, I heard the first *rev* of a Harley engine. It took reasoning, to guess that it wasn't coming from the baby stroller. I was keenly aware of it because I was preparing to write a chapter about thought.

Surely, we must *think*, in order to reason. And we must rationalize conflicting sensory inputs into a reality that reconciles them all. A mountain lion's roar means something very different if we are in the mountains rather than sitting on the couch watching TV.

And thus, we reason. We also wonder. We are trying to anticipate events that we cannot witness. Either, because we are not there, or because they haven't happened yet.

I wonder how many people will read these words I'm writing? If I write them this way, or *that*, will it affect the number of readers? I wonder who's reading the last four books I wrote. Or who would be reading them if I'd written them better.

We reason and we wonder. We also judge. Is this environment safe? What, if any, are the threats? Here is a judgment we've all been guilty of at some time or another:

"What's in it for me?"

Should we wear these clothes, or those? Which are the most flattering to our peers? Which suit or skirt will get us our way?

These are not complicated notions. How else would we choose a spouse, or a house, or a job? We reason, we wonder, we judge. And we imagine. Imagination is more complicated than the afore mentioned forms of thought, because those take into account only the *here and now*. To imagine, we must visualize. In doing so, we overlay transparent images on the *here and now*.

We see a bridge, where there is no bridge, in order to build a bridge. We imagine a person smiling or doing other things that we fancy. But these images are conjured, rather than *fetched*. They are tenuous and airy; without form or texture. But they'll do for contemplation's sake. You can't touch imaginary images. If you can, you are in trouble. We imagine, in hopes of the best, or to recognize the worst, if it ever comes to pass.

And then there is the self-talk; that whispering chatter of the committee and our heads. The little devil on my left shoulder argues with the little angel on my right. In the middle, we take both sides of the debate, in our own voice. When the self-talk starts, it's hard to stop.

I imagine that there are those who've never known a moment of quiet in their heads. Many of us have learned to quiet the voices and find peace. I know it is possible, because I found peace. Altruism gets us out of our own heads. Giving and caring puts the emphasis on someone other than ourselves.

And finally, there is prayer. In a conversation, directed at someone outside of ourselves. A telepathy, of sorts, with God - where we ask for and give thanks for his favor.

Meanwhile, back at mom's house, she's not supposed to be there. She's dead. But where is *there*? I believe, based upon empirical and personal self-experimentation, that, *that there and then* is a physical patch of neural real estate. It may be distributed or co-located, but each *then and there* are separate and distinct from some, but not *all* others.

My mother isn't supposed to exist, in any other *there and then*, after her death. But I go to that house, in that *there and then* so often that I'm pretty sure that it is permanently connected (neurologically speaking) to my ever transitioning *here and now*.

The house is connected, however tenuously, to me. And my mother, who lives on, in a large neural network in my brain, is tenuously connected to that house. And so we meet there, in fractured realities. Every time, adding more synaptic tendrils between worlds.

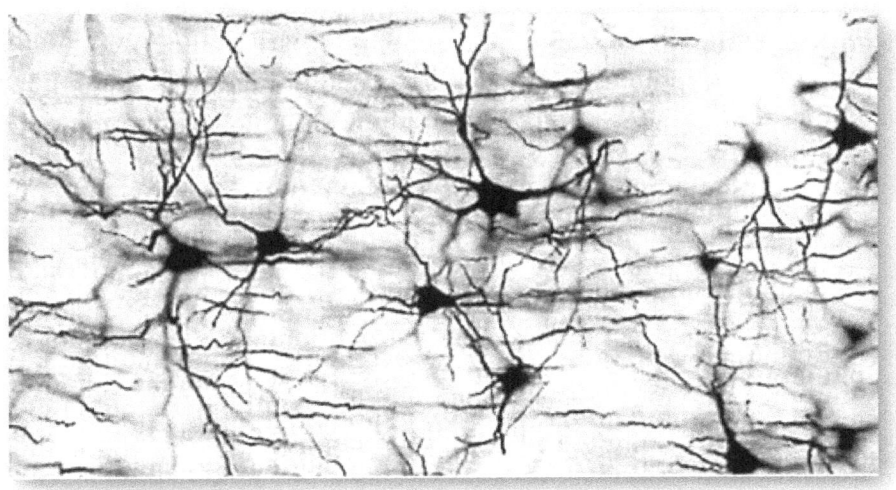

I had a friend who died too young. We used to meet in what I thought was a no man's land between the living and dead. Maybe there are parts of our brains that are sensitive enough to communicate with the micro-whispers of the dead. I won't go looking for close encounters of the ghost kind. I'm only interested in exploring my own mind. But really - how would I know the difference?

Suppose we are *touchable* by outside influences that tickle our neurons? It might be wise not to encourage such encounters. I've been *touched* many times, in decades past. But I wasn't running trials on my own brain until recently.

I should stop. But I'm hooked. I'm in the control phase. In the real world, I have very little power. I can't even fly, for crying out loud. I often counsel others, telling them they can't wrestle satisfaction out of the universe. The universe just won't allow it. How hypocritical of me? I'm trying to wrestle satisfaction from the universe between my ears.

Am I tampering with processes that are not meant to be controlled? Am I flirting with schizophrenia? Or, God forbid, opening my mind to external tampering? Maybe you should take this book as a warning. Where will I end up if I keep going; prison, an asylum? Or, in a self-induced coma, locked in without access to any outside stimulus? I can imagine even worse.

I have a moral compass in the *here and now*. Most of the time, it tells me right from wrong. During those times, I try to see my fellow human beings as I think God does. His children, myself included, are all branches of the same family tree.

At other times, when my sinful nature guides my consciousness, I see objects of my desire, and I see competition. I feel convicted already. So, before you get all sanctimonious, let me remind you that you do the same thing.

You creep through crowded parking lots, just like I do. And you lurk on that car pulling out, so you can grab that parking space before your competition, in the other car, turns the corner. I have you laughing now - right?

But it doesn't stop there. What about that last dinner roll or doughnut? And oh my God, don't we lose our entire minds on the greediest day of the American year? *Black Friday* starts on the same day we give thanks for what we already have.

World-wide, greed drives the business of sports. Get the ball and you'll get paid more money. First place wins the prize; even if the competition dies in the process. The prettiest girl gets the guy, even if it's only to spoil the competition's chances. The richest guy gets the prettiest girl, just to toy with her and throw her away. His competition would have cherished her for life. We, as a species, fight over things we don't even want; like an insignificant patch of land on a deserted island in a world war.

Having made my point - back to *my* brain. I am aware of my moral compass. I know right from wrong. I hold myself accountable for my actions. I even try to police my thought life during my waking hours. I have friends, family and acquaintances that are real people. It would be wrong for me to harm them.

Oh, but how easy it is to justify bad behavior in dreamland. None of the people are real. I can do whatever I want - right? There is no one there to hurt, but me. And that is precisely the nature of my paradox. In a world where there is no real competition, I can take whatever I want. But I am taking *whatever I want*, from a construct of my own mind.

And what prize could possibly be worth competing for in a dream? Have you ever received money in a dream? Weren't you sorely disappointed, when you opened your eyes and watched it vanish into thin air? Material gains (in dreams) mean nothing in the real world. One-ups-man-ship, in a dream, might make for a good chuckle when you wake up.

But there is a treasure that bridges the gap into consciousness. The warm glow of pleasure lingers on for hours. The currency of pleasure is Dopamine. And it spends, on either side of the border of consciousness, in any of a thousand dreamscapes.

Dopamine is one of three neurotransmitters that regulate brain activity by closing, or opening the synaptic gates between neurons.

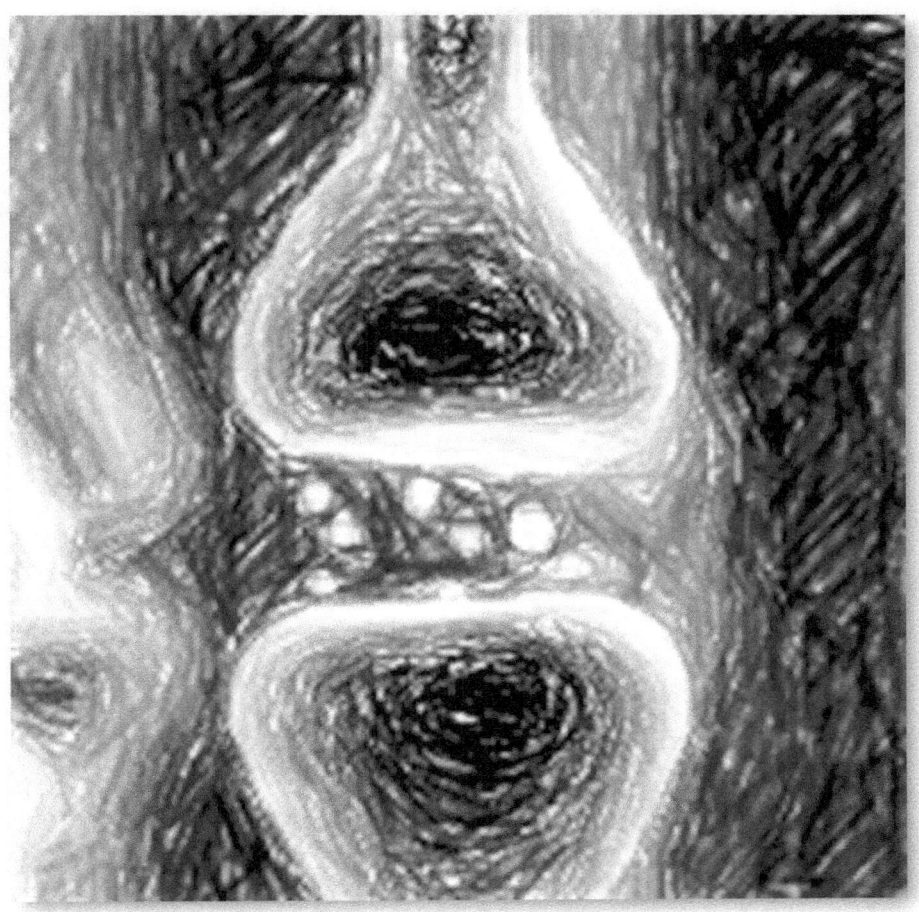

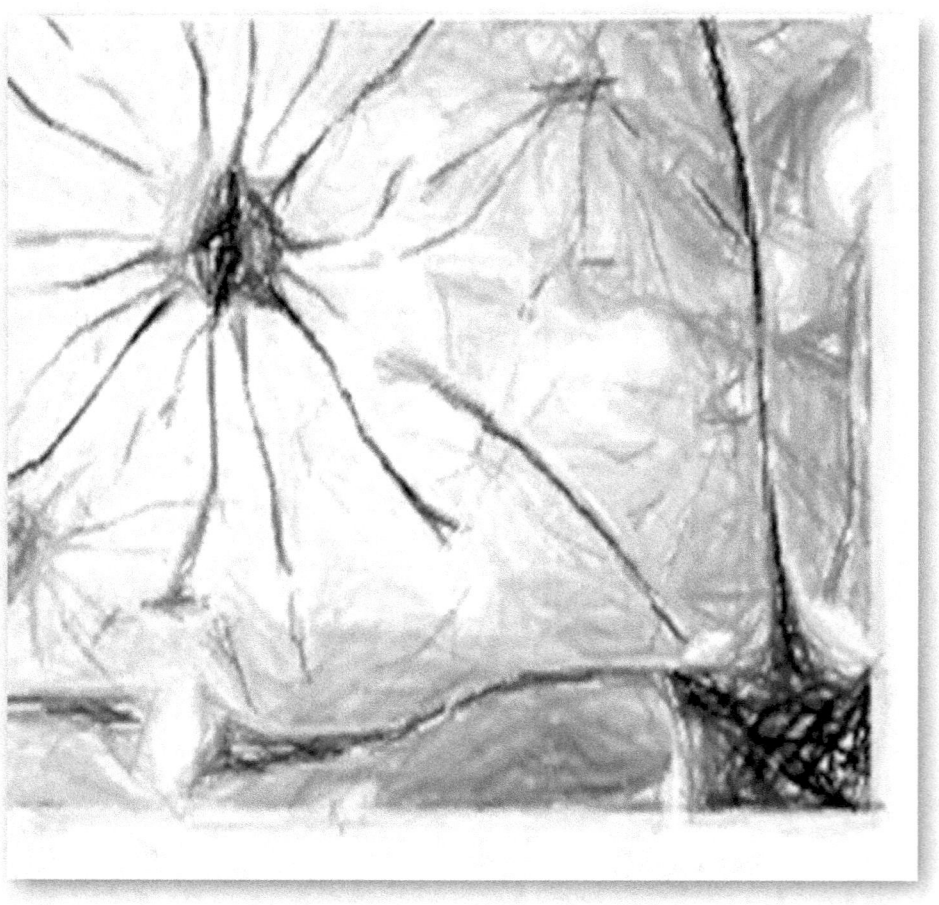

Dopamine, Serotonin, and Norepinephrine are molecular keys that fit into the *gate locks* of the pathways that each of the three control. Those locks are called receptors. Dopamine molecules fit into Dopamine receptors. Serotonin and norepinephrine molecules will not fit into Dopamine receptors. Each of the three fit, uniquely into their own receptors. Each of the three, uniquely or in combination, control the various aspects of our behavior.

Dopamine is the key to reward incentivized behavior. Specific to this conversation, Dopamine is the key to the pleasure pathways. It is Dopamine that fuels our desires. And it is Dopamine that gives us the warm glow of pleasure. Dopamine provides our drive for pleasure, and it is its own reward.

Those that crave chocolate can trade one bite for a shot of Dopamine to one of the pleasure centers. Think chocolate is girlie? Replace it with bacon. Alcohol activates Dopamine gates in the pleasure network. Drugs, like crack cocaine and methamphetamine fit perfectly into our Dopamine receptors. They trigger all the pleasure centers in the system at one time, producing a period of ecstasy. Use them often enough and your brain will stop making Dopamine. At that point you choose the drug at all costs. Family, job, home - all become secondary priorities. Some lose all - including their lives.

The only thing in the natural world that triggers simultaneous firing of all the pleasure centers is sexual climax. Dopamine naturally drives us to want sex, even before the first time we experience climax. God put the sex drive in us. The reproductive urge, in importance, comes right after staying alive. Self-preservation is the first law of nature. Preservation of the species is the second law.

Ah, but once we experience climax, we are (in a sense) branded for life. Sex is the only activity in our natural arsenal that produces absolute and total bliss. And, unlike most of the animal kingdom, humans don't have a season of heat. Humans are always hot. Sex drives entire industries; from fashion, to perfume and cologne, to cosmetics, pornography and plastic surgery. We all want to be sexy.

Sexy is cute and acceptable. We throw the word around as if we were talking about soda pop flavors. But deep in the core of our brains, sex is a primordial battle urge, the fulfillment of which will eliminate the competition's genetic progeny from the gene pool. Sex is a wild and primitive urge to promote our own likeness, in the jungle of competition.

When a woman out dresses her friend, what she's really saying is "die bitch". Deep in a man's brain, he wants to be the father of the entire next generation. Our deep and intimate primal appetites are covered over by a thin veil called civilization. Strip away that veil and we become savage. A better word might be psychotic.

A s a teenager and a young adult, I sometimes had erotic dreams, that went *all the way*. An older mentor once told a group of us teenaged boys that *wet dreams* were natural.

"It's gonna come out, one way or another," he told us.

Sometimes I didn't know it had happened, until I woke up...wet. I seem to remember being embarrassed at those occurrences; like I was when I peed the bed as a child. I hadn't had a dream like that, since I was in my thirties. That is, not until a few months ago, during the control phase of my lucid dream research.

I was touring the office area of something like a library or school campus. I remember seeing books. But my attention was on the middle-aged woman behind a counter of some sort. I fancied her a librarian. She wore glasses. And her mousy brown hair was slightly *tossed*. She gave me a *come hither* glance, as I passed the counter. I told her to:

"Take me in *there*." Referring to an empty office, opposite the counter.

I was in control. She had to comply.

"Close the door."

She did. And then she pleasured me. Now, mind you, I have a pleasant dream from time to time. But they haven't ended in climax for decades. And I've never been in control, until *that* night.

I was in control. She seemed willing...enough. It seemed innocent. After all, it was just a dream. But it was a *lucid* dream, with all the sensory input of a real sexual encounter. The librarian took me all the way to the Dopamine jackpot. My brain lit up like the heating elements in an electric toaster. The sensation spread through all the pleasure centers of my brain. I more than felt it - I saw it. A warm infrared glow spread through my brain, like a mushroom cloud.

But the pleasure center bingo was accompanied by a sense of guilt. The same guilt I would have felt if I'd done the deed in real life. She was willing though - wasn't she? She'd given me *the eye*. I know the look. But she wasn't real. The act shouldn't have had any consequences. But it did - because I have a conscience.

This leap in lucid dream control was going to remain a secret, between me and God. I never saw the librarian again. *That*, was a one night stand. But I knew right away that I was going to try it again. I woke up with a warm glow. And the internal *and external* stains of sin.

The next dream girl wasn't so willing. She didn't give me a come-hither look. I said the word *girls*, and a crowd of young women appeared in the construct of my choosing ground. (In a subsequent experiment, I changed the *girls* to *women*. And the same young women put on thirty years and fifty pounds, right before my eyes. I changed them back.)

I chose a young woman and told her to, "Follow me."

Oddly, the other women warned her.

"No. Don't go with him."

She tried to resist my *spell*, but she didn't really have a choice. I separated her from the crowd and led her into an empty room. I closed the door behind us. She did as I wished her to. But we were interrupted by my guilty conscience.

The next time, I didn't even bother commanding. I just took a woman by the hand and led her, like a lamb to the slaughter. Other women pulled her by her other arm, and kept her from me. I wanted to pull that Dopamine lever, in the worst way. But it just didn't feel *right*. As my assaults grew bolder, men would intercede on my intended victims' behalf. I'd become a predator in my own brain. And my brain sent out agents, to stop me.

One night, I learned something new. I saw a woman walking toward her house, on a city block.

"Can I come in with you?"

The woman looked at me like I was crazy.

"Hell no, you can't come in with me!"

Wow, this was new. So, I experimented to see if there was a difference, in response, between *asking* and *telling*. There certainly was. If I asked, and they said no, and I then commanded, and they complied - that's sorta like rape. I knew I was in trouble. My brain was protecting itself. But from what?

Now let's go back to the reception area I talked about in chapter two. Here's what really happened. Picture a large factory with two acres of floor space. It was big enough to assemble jet airliners. But they weren't building airliners. I couldn't tell what they were building. But something, or some things were being put together there. Parts and pieces came in. Complex products went out.

There were intersecting aisles, high and wide. A youngish work force, male and female, went about their business in workspaces on both sides of each aisle. I shouldn't have been there, but it made a good dreamscape for my experiments.

"Girls," I ordered.

And young women strode into the aisles. I was about to choose, when an amplified female voice, robotic in tone, made an announcement.

"All personnel - evacuate the area."

Young men and young women walked, at a normal pace, toward the exits. My brain saw *me* (the conscious me) as an unwelcome predator.

"I repeat - all personnel evacuate the area."

When the last person was gone, the overhead lights began to dim.

"This facility is shutting down - *period*."

The facility went totally dark, and I begged:

"Wait. I'll be good."

Lights ramped up and pedestrian traffic resumed. Two licentious female characters floated above the workspace.

"We are willing," one of them cooed.

Then the other seductress added:

"We will do as you wish, if you acknowledge that we are from Satan."

I ignored them after thinking it through. But I'd learned that this battle for pleasure had ramifications that I hadn't earlier considered. Since I was there, I might as well learn more.

"Does this factory represent my brain?"

"No silly. This is just the reception area."

"If this place represents the reception area, then how big is my brain?"

"The size of a city."

"Are you saying that I have a, city-sized, brain under my control?"

"There are parts of it that control you."

But there was additional dialog I didn't tell you in chapter two.

"If you keep this up," one of four women told me. "We're going to show up in the real world."

I got cold chills and goosebumps, as I asked:

"How will I know the difference?"

My heart surely skipped a beat, when they laughed, and she answered:

"You won't."

A group of young men laughed as they mopped one of the workspace floors. Two of them teased me, after hearing the girl's warning.

"Go ahead. Keep it up."

"That's right. Keep on...stupid."

I woke up, with foreboding on my tongue.

"I went too far this time. Oh God, I went too far."

My wife shook me.

"I'm here, baby. I'm here. Come back."

Thank God. I was in my own bed, with my wife standing over me, in our little square house that I love so much.

As near as I can figure, from research done after I woke up, I was in the thalamus - *my* thalamus, the nerve center of my brain. Thalamus comes from a Greek word that means *chamber*. It may be thought of, as sort of an information hub. The thalamus acts as a switchboard, relaying sensory inputs from receptors in different parts of the body, i.e:

"No, silly. This is just the reception area."

Experts believe that the thalamus determines which impulses, from various channels, are to be relayed to their corresponding processing areas. Visual input, for example, is received from the retina, via the optic nerve. Those inputs are preprocessed in the thalamus and routed to the visual cortex, for storage as raw data, and processed into images. Sight, sound, touch and taste (all but smell) are preprocessed in the thalamus.

The thalamus also regulates states of sleep, consciousness, and arousal. The whole brain is active while we're dreaming. Researchers believe that dreams are a function of the reticular activating system, whose circuits run from the brain stem, through the thalamus, to the cerebral cortex. Consciousness (our ego) lives in the cerebral cortex. That's why dreams seem real.

I believe, from my own experimentation, that the thalamus is the *dream factory*, where sensory information is *fetched* from the various memory storage area's and put together into dream sequences and characters. I (my ego) is supposed to operate in the cerebral cortex, where my dreams are lived out. I am not, according to the dream factory operations manager (the amplified female voice), supposed to be in the thalamus making conscious decisions in the dream construction process.

Furthermore, I am not supposed to be in the heads of imaginary dream characters. And I most certainly shouldn't have power over their actions. In a sense, I'm trying to force my brain to have sex with itself, in an attempt to trick the pleasure center into believing I'm having sex with a real woman. This is the very definition of *mental masturbation*.

And what would happen, if I could pull it off? My brains operations managers know what would happen. That's why they're trying to stop me. The experts believe that damage to the thalamus can lead to permanent coma. I've been warned. I should stop, before I break my brain and end up stuck in limbo with my delusions.

My mother will probably be there scolding me. I'd be forever telling her about the new wife that I love. And our little square house on the hill that I'll never see again. The young people from the dream factory will be there laughing at me. Telling me:
"We told you so."

I might eventually give in to those two, devilish succubuses. And be lost to the dark side. I better stop, while there's still time.

I couldn't take it anymore - the guilt, I mean. I shared my dark secret with a trusted friend.

"I'm trying to make my brain have sex with itself."

"*Dude* - that's deep," he said. "But I have no idea what you're talking about."

I was kind of relieved.

"Never mind, bro. It's complicated."

Confessing to an acquaintance who had no idea what I was talking about wasn't good enough. So, I came clean…with my wife.

She listened intently while I explained how dopamine worked. I told her my theories about the thalamus and the dream factory. But what she heard was that I was a rapist in training.

"You have to stop," she told me with finality.

She sounded like the operations manager at the dream factory:

"This facility is shutting down - *period.*"

Then my wife asked:

"When do you see your psychiatrist?"

"I see Doctor Wilson next month."

"You have to tell him to take you off the medication that's causing your lucid dreams."

And then she cried.

"Aren't I good enough?

"Of course, you are. They're just experiments," I lied.

Sex in the real world is complicated. It takes physical exertion and stamina. And then there's foreplay. Real women aren't microwave ovens. There's no foreplay required in a dreamscape. No dating ritual, no dinner; simply self-gratification.

But then I thought; since she already knows, maybe she could help me connect sex in the real world to my Dopamine experiments.

"Hey babe. Maybe you can help me with my next experiment?"

"Really? You want me to participate in your fantasy bullshit?"

She gave in - halfheartedly. But that was enough to light up my pleasure centers. I went to sleep with that warm glow.

I didn't expect what happened. The dreamscape characters (including myself) were bent out of shape - pissed off that my wife (in the real world) had used up all the dopamine. The dope house (Dopamine house) across the street from Mom's house got paved over with a parking lot.

I'd managed, in the past, to get a smidge of that heroin and trick my brain into releasing Serotonin. Heroin, you see, is a key that fits the serotonin locks. And my reward for tricking my brain into releasing serotonin was a slight narcotic high, that triggered a small release of Dopamine.

But not this night. My mother was angry too. Maybe she scored some dopamine every time I visited that heroin dealer. The succubuses cursed me out. The willing, of the female persuasion, slammed doors in my face. So, my assumption was correct. Dopamine is currency in both worlds. The living world and the dream world were at odds, in a battle to control the Dopamine supply.

Since I wasn't doing anything nasty, I took the opportunity to question more of the characters that came out of the dream factory. I ran into a family friend, and her son. They were there - with all the texture of living beings. I questioned her.

"Are you real?"

"Of course."

"Are you autonomous?"

"Yes."

Ok, I thought - I'll throw her a curve.

"How many children do you have?"

Since there was one child standing there (I guess), she answered:

"One."

But I knew she had three children. So, I corrected her.

"You have three children."

And then I asked again.

"How many children do you have?"

She answered:

"Three."

Good, I thought. I'll throw in a few diversion questions and came back to it latter. I learned that from my psychiatrist.

"How many children do you have?"

"Twelve," she answered.

Then she turned around and climbed a tree.

They didn't have much of a mind, I decided when I woke up. But maybe I can teach them. And by doing so, give them their own neural networks. As of now, they were independent, but not autonomous. I'll teach them, every chance I get. What could possibly go wrong? Right?

I read all day, that day. I had to figure out how to increase the supply of Dopamine. Out of a hundred billion brain cells, only four hundred thousand produce Dopamine. I found out I could take the amino acid precursor to Dopamine; L-Tyrosine. Our brains synthesize Dopamine from L-Tyrosine. I cut down on coffee and didn't eat sweets that day. I also took the second allowable pill in my daily Bupropion prescription. Bupropion is a Dopamine re-uptake inhibitor. It keeps Dopamine from migrating back to the producer cells, giving the user an increased sense of wellbeing.

I think I over did it. I came to, in the first-class lounge of a Boeing 747. *Wow, that was a great nap*, I thought, as I noticed concern on the faces of the flight attendants. The plane shuddered. The flight crew freaked. The captain called an emergency. I ran for my seat, but it was too late.

Now, might be a good time to tell you about my *tell*. A *tell* is something a lucid dreamer uses to distinguish dream life from reality. My lucid dreams are so real, I have to verify that I am indeed dreaming. Here's my *tell*. If I can jump in the air and stay there, I know I'm dreaming. I use the *tell* at least once a night. I usually have more than one dream, per slumber. And I nap often.

Now, back to the 747 that's in a nose down spin. With every revolution, the ground gets closer, outside the starboard windows. I know, from personal experience (I used to be a pilot), that when a plane is falling, the passengers become weightless. That's how they film those zero-gravity space movies; in a diving plane.

Yeah, so I'm floating in the lounge cabin. Everything not nailed down is floating too. I can see buildings getting larger with every spin. And I can't use the *tell* because I'm *supposed* to be floating. Oh God, this might be the reality in my dream research. I have no reason to believe it's not really happening. So, what do I do?

I pray out loud, as if I really am about to die. It'll be all over in a few more spins. And then we hit. But I've never been in a plane crash. I have no idea how it's supposed to feel. My brain *fetches* the best jolt it can come up with. I leave the wreckage. Just before it goes up in a giant fireball.

Way too much Dopamine. I won't do that again. But what a ride. The next day I asked my wife if we could stay in our little square house today. So we chilled and enjoyed each other's company.

That evening we watched TV. I flipped briefly to a local news channel, while my wife went to use the bathroom.

"Have you seen this man?"

There was a pencil sketch of a man in the cutaway shot. I had no reason to look.

"He is thought to be the man that sexually assaulted a woman in a Midtown bookstore. The police said that a man fitting this description forced her into an office and..."

I turned the channel so my wife didn't hear it. Why would I do that - turn the channel I mean? Cold chills shot down my spine.

Later that night, I tried to make love to my wife. Nothing happened. It was as if my arousal mechanism was broken. Remember - arousal is governed by the thalamus. The dream girls laughed and pointed that night. One went with another guy. And the two of them laughed at me before they shut the door. This was an easy *fetch*. It wasn't the first time a girl told her friends I couldn't perform.

I tried to have sex with my wife the next night. Nothing happened. I tried, the night after that, and the night after that. Nights turned into weeks. I had broken something in the dream factory that night when I went too far. I even prayed, to no avail. I could hear those four girls, from the dream factory, laughing when I asked how I would know the difference between reality and fantasy.

"You won't."

And the guys.

"Go ahead. Keep it up."

"Stupid."

The dream factory was broken. But the succubuses chased me through the nights. And my arousal mechanism was broken. I made excuses to my wife. Eventually, we stopped trying. After a while, the police were still hunting the 'Midtown rapist'.

"At the top of the news tonight, the search goes on for the Midtown rapist. This man..."

Who looked just like me.

"...has assaulted two women. One, in a Midtown bookstore. And another, on the campus of Midtown Junior College. He has, on three separate occasions, tried to drag young women away from their friends. And this, on the Midtown Junior College campus, where he raped his second victim.

My wife works from dawn, past dusk. By the time she comes home, it's usually almost time for bed. I bide my time with reading, writing and theoretical research while she's away. One night, at a typical late dinner, she asked:

"Honey, what have you been up to lately?"

"You know - the usual."

"No sweetie, I don't. We're newlyweds, remember?"

"Well…" And I chose my words carefully, while choosing the best piece of steak. "I read a lot, write a little, and then there is my scientific research."

She slammed down her fork.

"Are you talking about your silly ass dream girls?"

I sat speechless, while she went on.

"I am so f'ing over this. You better get over it too, or I'm gonna be over *you*."

As if things couldn't get any worse, she tossed a newspaper on the table. Did she pull it out of her bra, or what?

"Have you seen this?"

I didn't even have to look.

"That again?"

""Yes, that! Here - I'll read it to you. A man fitting the description of the Midtown rapist was spotted, stalking women outside of the Midtown Ford Motors assembly plant, last week. Four young women reported him to their supervisor, who subsequently called police. And, I quote:

"He tried to strike up a conversation with us, but we just kept walking."

"Oh my God…" one of them reported. "we had no idea it was the Midtown rapist.""

I wanted in the worst way, to change the subject.

"I don't know why you're so hung up on that guy? Do you have some rape baggage you haven't told me about?"

Not a great way to change the subject. The slap came without warning.

"Are you crazy? Why'd you slap me?"

"*Me*? Am *I* crazy? Look at this picture, you asshole."

My eyes betrayed my confusion.

"Come on, it's just a coincidence. You couldn't, in a million years, think that's me."

She didn't come to bed with me that night. But those two vamps from the dream factory did.

"Why are you *fetching* the unwilling, when you can get everything you want right here baby?"

I tried my best to ignore them. I did everything short of calling on the Lord, to stay out of their devilish clutches.

"Leave me alone - please."

"Why should we, when your wife can't satisfy you?"

I closed my dream eyes, hoping there'd be different women floating there when I opened them.

"Come on," one of them whispered. "Be a sport. You know you want to."

I opened my dream eyes as she was still undressing.

"No. Stop. That's not what I want. It's not who I am."

Before I knew it, I had her by the throat, bashing her head against the factory wall.

If I could only remember my wife's phone number. The mortgage is paid. She'll let me in.

I woke up in a cold sweat, at home, in our little square house on the hill. I rolled over to look for my wife. But the sun was already up. She's probably gone to work by now.

I got up and started a pot of coffee. My wife usually made the morning pot. But she was probably still upset about that crap in the news. Over coffee, I laid out my plans for the day. First, I'd read. Then I'd write a little. And finally, I'd do some Internet research. Maybe this would be the day, that I would figure out how to fix my thalamus.

So, let's see…where do I start? Will it be Sigmund Freud or C.S. Lewis. Morning bled into noon, as I read. Afternoon bled into the evening, as I wrote. It must have been around 6pm when I logged onto the Internet for research. And it was right there, at the opening page, where I catch up on the national and world news.

My picture took up most of the page. On top of it, in bold red letters, read the words:
   "Midtown Rapist Murders Prostitute Outside of Strip Club."
   I slammed my laptop so hard, that I was sure I broke it.

Damn! There's the garage door motor. She's going to say something, I just know it. Calm down, I told myself. Pretend to be normal. I had to chuckle out loud at that one - at normal. Pretend you're not crazy. Open the door with a smile.

I opened the door with a smile all right. Until I was tackled by a wall of blue uniforms. I hit my head on the floor so hard that I saw stars. Okay, so maybe it's a dream. Use the *tell*. But I couldn't with the weight of four cops on top of me. It had to be a dream. They were reading me my rights, I think. But I couldn't really tell, because my wife was screaming over their voices.

"You piece of shit! How could you? You crazy, selfish bastard. I knew it was you. I knew it."

What's she doing in my dream? She's supposed to be in the *here and now*. How'd she get in the dream factory? They *said* I wouldn't be able to tell the difference. The setting sun revealed a fleet of police cars. My neighbors all stood outside with their mouths agape.

"Watch your head, sir," a cop told me as he smashed me into the back of his cruiser.

This *has* to be a dream. But man - these handcuffs sure feel real. Cops with notepads questioned my neighbors as I was driven away. My wife never came out of the house. That made sense; she wasn't supposed to be there anyway.

All the way to the police station, I read the street signs, trying to find a flaw in the dreamscape. The dream factory was back in action. And this time it had outdone itself. The cops in the front seat didn't talk. I'm sure I would have found a flaw in their conversation, if they had. We pulled into the Midtown police precinct parking lot, with a sea of blue and red, spinning lights behind us.

I could feel the heat from the news crews' floodlights. I'm pretty sure I saw that lady that reports the Channel 9 News. They took me out of the car; an officer on each side, with an arm under my handcuffed elbows. I reminded myself to use the *tell*. I picked my feet up off the ground, and sure enough, I stayed in the air.

"You do know you guys are from the dream factory, don't you?"

They didn't answer.

"Let me go, or I'll make you disappear."

A reporter shoved a microphone in my face.

"Are you the Midtown rapist?"
At this point, my anger was on autopilot.
"Get away from me, you bitch. Or I'll make you disappear too."
I yelled at the entire construct,
"Can't you see me floating?"

And then I realized that those two cops were carrying me. My head reeled, with the realization that this might actually be reality. Of all the possibilities of realities to wake up to, which one could possibly be worse than being a serial rapist and a murderer?

I wouldn't walk, so they dragged me through the police station, past the silent stares of hardened cops. They dragged me into an interrogation room and slammed me down on a metal chair. What reality could possibly be worse?

"Shut up and sit back down!"

"Okay, okay - wait, Gimme a minute. I was just… You guys *just* dragged me in here."

"Nobody dragged you in here. I don't have all night, Walter. So, what's it gonna be. You came in here, *voluntarily*, to talk. So, talk."

"Look - I can't do this. Those guys are maniacs."

"Where you gonna go, Walter. Go ahead - there's the door."

"Okay detective. Strap in. And I'll tell you what we did last night. I'll tell you; but I won't name names. I just need to get this one off my chest. And who else am I gonna tell.

We caught a guy wearing a wire. We both know who the guy is…I mean, was."

"Who is we?"

"We found one of your wireless bugs, in his pocket, with some *real* quarters. You guys are stupid. You gotta switch it up sometimes.

Are you listening, detective Peete? We snatched your guy out the back way; right under your noses, and drove him to his own meat market. You know those metal tables they use to cut through sides of beef? The ones with a band-saw at one end?".

"Yeah, I know the ones."

"Well I'd never seen a table like that before last night. And it turned my stomach when they slammed him down on it. You know why?"

"I don't know, Walter. Why don't you tell me?"

"Gimme a cigarette.....Ahhh...the menthol."

They turned on the saw, while he laid there begging for his life. But here's the kicker. They never laid a finger on him. They just dared him to move. And he didn't. Then they flipped the switch that started the table moving.

"Your snitch would rather die on that table, than be tortured by those psychos."
"What psychos?"
"Come on, Peete; stop interrupting. So the guy lays there grimacing, while the table pushes him head first into that band-saw. I thought for sure he'd jump off the table; we all did. But he just twitched a little...until the blade disappeared in the top of his head."

The guy was laying in the fetal position. So next it cut through his arms. They turned it off, after it cut his legs off.

You know what happened then? They chopped through his neck with a meat cleaver. None of us wanted to touch what was left. Blood ran off the table like a warm slurpy.
Hahahaha haaa hahaha.

And then two of those sick bastards put his head back together, and wrapped it up in meat paper. They taped it closed, like it was a pot roast. They made me put it out in the store front, for some square to take home for dinner.
Go see for yourselves. It's right there in that assholes meat market, on the corner of Sixth and Main."

"Please turn off the recorder, Doctor Wilson."
"Did they read you your rights, Walt?"
"It's Walter. And I don't care about that legal crap. Anyway, that was thirteen years ago. I said at the trial that I didn't remember. They couldn't protect me. My only way out was death row."

"You done?"

"Yeah."

"Tell me about the incident with your appeals lawyer...Miss Cushionberry."

Boy, was she pretty - real pretty. But I was a fifty-year-old death row inmate. And I'd just gotten my front tooth pulled, the day before. Believe it or not, I was embarrassed.

"Let's start with your nick-name." She looked down at her notebook. "Psycho Michael. How'd you come by that?"

I smiled, because it was a funny story. That's when she saw my missing tooth.

"Really? That's what you wanna talk about?"

She nodded.

"Okay, that was back in Detroit. While everybody else was sellin drugs, me and my boy, Al, was makin bank selling fake gold and diamonds to small business owners. Mostly tire and auto body shops. So, we're working the block, lookin for suckers. We go in this body shop where they were bumpin a dent out of this Rolls Royce. Al gave me the look. This was the one.

Before you know it, Al has us in the back with this Italian lookin mutha fu..."

"Mister Harris! I'm a Christian."

She didn't like my cursing.

"Sorry, Miss Cushionberry."

And I really meant it.

"So we're runnin the scam on this dude named Sal. We're just two ghetto lowlifes with some hot gold coins. After Sal tested the real coins, Al switched his acid vial with a vial full of water."

"How's that?"

"It's like this pretty lady. The acid only comes in two types of vials. We had both kinds..."

"Already filled with water."

She got it; and slipped me an unintended smile. And I had *her* too. She completed my sentence. I can spot peoples 'tells' in a New York minute. And I've never even been to New York. A New York minute is only a second in Detroit.

"Right."

I slipped her a quick smile back. But I didn't put too much on it, because of my dental condition.

""So we handed the dude the whole bag of fake Golden Eagles and pocketed the real ones. We're on our way out the rollup door, when Al starts lookin down at his shoes. And I'm wonderin' what's wrong with this fool.

"Hey!" This guy yells from across the shop. "That moolie is a con man."

So I whip out my Glock 21, from my fake fat belly, and fire a shot in the air, so we can make a run for my car. The shot hits the overhead hoist, and the whole thing falls on the hood of that Silver Shadow.

"Oops."

By now there's chop shop goons comin out of the woodwork.

"What're you waitin on," Al yells. "Shoot somebody!""

Me and the pretty lawyer both laughed.

"So, they beat the crap out of us and called the cops. But the gun they gave the cops was a chrome plated 1911."

"They gave the cops a different gun, and kept yours?"

She shouldn't have used the word *cops*. I had her speaking my language.

"Right. So, I copped to attempted robbery. The gunshot put me in prison. Sal, and them, turned out to be the wrong guys to mess with. They were connected. If I told the cops about the gun swap, they would've told the DA that I shot at *them*."

Miss Cushionberry nodded. "Attempted murder."

""Before you know it, I'm in the pen with hardened criminals, and I never even been to Juvi. First day in the chow hall and all these dudes is muggin me. When I hear,

"Mike! Is that you?"

See; when I was a kid, my family called me by my middle name, to distinguish me from my gangster uncle, Walter. He was Walter - I was Mike. So the guys in the neighborhood knew me as Mike.

So I look over and its Derrick, mutha fu. Excuse me. It's Derrick Peyton. There was so many Peyton brothers that they called our neighborhood, Peyton Place. You know, after that old daytime soap.""

But she didn't know.

"So what happened?"

""Derrick called me over, to sit with him and his two brothers, Will and Freddy. Now Derrick had always taken a liking to me, because I was smart - like him. The pervs didn't try me that night, cause they thought I was a Peyton boy.

Next day at chow, Derrick whispers to me,

"Reach over and snatch my dessert."

And I look at him like, *'I ain't snatchin your dessert.'* And he gives me the, *'Just do what I said'* look. So, I reached over and snatched his Jello. And he throws up his hands like I really took it. Okay cool - for one more night.

Next day, we're in line and Derrick says:

"See that nigga over there, muggin you?"

I go, "Yeah, I see him."

"He's gonna try to take your manhood. We can't protect you from that. You're gonna have to drop his ass, like a hot rock."

Later on that day, the pervert hemmed me up in a corner and looked down at me like I was a fourteen year old girl, and says:

"We can do this the easy way; or we can do it the hard way."

So, I look at this nigga like; *'oh really?'*

And then he said the magic words.

"Go ahead; take your best…"

He didn't even get *'shot'* out of his mouth. I was more mad than scared. I don't like being embarrassed. So, I reached up; and this nigga was tall.'"

"Mister Harris; please?"

"He was a tall man. I reached up with my left hand, to grab the back of his head, so I could smack him in the jaw with my right."

"You were going to slap him?"

Her eyes widened; like, 'How was that going to stop me from getting plucked.'

"I'll get to that later. My timing was a little off."

I raised my hands to show her.

""My left palm hit near the back of his head, at the same time my right palm hit his jaw. We all heard the *'snap, crackle, pop.'*

"Oops."

The look on my face must'a been weirder than the stupid one on *his*; with his head layin on his left shoulder. And he just fell over.'"

"Oh my God; you snapped his neck?"

"Broke his jaw too."

"Where'd you learn a move like that?"

"Like I told you -I was smart. I took advanced math in high school. I hung out with the only Chinese kid in the whole school. For a year and a half, he taught me something called Wing Chun."

"What's that?"

"Kung fu. But I was never that good at it."

"How very eclectic of you."

""All the brothers backed me up. They said it was self-defense. For the next three weeks, they all kidded me. They would bow down when I passed, and say,

"Let Psycho Michael through.""

Three weeks later, I got out on a technicality."

"What happened to Al?"

"They didn't need a pro; they needed a patsy. Al got probation. He split the scene, right after telling me that the mob had killed somebody with *my* gun. And that's how I first got owned."

She closed her notebook.

"You didn't write anything."

She ignored me.

"Guard - I'm done here. I'll be back on Thursday, Walter."

"**A**nd Miss Cushionberry saw you every Tuesday and Thursday? For how many years?"

"Three or four, Doc. What difference does it make? We've been over all this before. And what are you scribbling today?"

"Never mind that, Walter. Would you like to comment on the police recording?"

"You've played that tape, every month, for the past year. I don't like hearing it any more this time, than I did the last. It hurts my soul to think I could have ever been that cruel. That was thirteen years ago. I haven't been that guy for a long time.

Kotrin Sully hadn't done anything to be killed so viciously. He paid his protection bill. It was the police, threatening to deport his Mexican common-law wife, that got him killed. The mob got wind of it and threatened to kill her, if Kotrin cooperated with the police. Poor guy got caught in the crossfire when the police told him they'd make it *look* like he cooperated, if he didn't.

Once his wife was murdered, he had no reason to fight. He laid on that table and took, what he thought, was due punishment for not protecting her. The death penalty is *my* due punishment, for not protecting *him*.

We both know I'm not crazy, Doctor Wilson. Stop trying to take me back to that murderous state of mind. I could've stopped it - if I'd had a heart."

The doctor nodded thoughtfully.

"If we can show that your heart was surgically removed through the manipulation of a criminal organization - that would be grounds for a stay of execution, based on insanity. We must provide the governor with a compelling argument that, *at the time*, you didn't know right from wrong."

"I'm tired, Doctor; real tired. I don't want a stay of execution."

He's gonna ignore me again. I see it in his eyes.

"I see something in you worth saving Walter. We *have* to try. I know that your uncle Walter played a big part in molding your former character. Can you tell me more about him?"

I might as well answer. He's just gonna sit there scribbling, if I don't.

"First of all, nobody called him Walter. He wouldn't allow it. Everybody called him 'Wack.'"

"Does the name 'Wack' carry any significance?"

"It did. He died a few years back. There were plenty of stories about how he got that name. The most obvious being that Uncle Wack was wacko."

"Did he suffer from mental illness?"

"No Doc - not at all. He was cool and calculating. He let people think he wasn't all there, so they would underestimate him. That was his con. He'd reel them in by seeming like an easy mark. But God help them when he flipped the switch. The man had ice water running through his veins.

Uncle Walter was a heroin supplier, on the side. But mainly he ran big cons - all over the country. He stretched his profit margin by leaving his dealers, with product already cut (or wacked) as far as it could be, without customers complaining. Some say his dealers gave him the name, Wack.

Personally, I think he got that name because people who crossed him disappeared; like Jimmy Hoffa, they got *wacked*.

"Thanks for bailin me out, Uncle Walter"

Uncle Walter checked me with that Barry White baritone.

"What'd I tell you about using my real name?"

As if everybody, including the cops, didn't know that Wack's real name was Walter Harris Junior.

"How'd your stupid ass pick Big Sal and them to try to run game on?"

"Dumb luck I guess. My boy, Al is from outta town. He didn't know who they were either."

We got in my uncles brand new, baby blue El Dorado. He tipped the parking lot attendant big, and peeled out onto Beaubien Boulevard.

"I heard they switched pistols on you."

I shook my head.

"You know they own you now - right?"

I was so naïve.

"How's that?"

"They're gonna use it for a hit. If anything comes back on them, you'll be the patsy. Oldest trick in the book."

I should've known I was about to be played like a pawn.

"I'm gonna help you out, nephew. We're gonna kill two birds, with one stone."

Here it comes.

"I owe a few favors down at the DA's office. The *man* is up for re-election. And he needs convictions. We all gotta put some skin in the game."

"Whoa, Wack. Who is *we*? And whose skin are you talkin about?"

"Look, Mike; you're gonna need an air tight alibi, when they use that gun. You're gonna plead guilty to attempted robbery. You ain't gonna walk, cause you fired a shot. You do a couple months in Jackson..."

"Hold up Unc..."

"No. *You* hold up. I got you the right attorney. And the DA is in the bag. You'll be out right after the election."

"Suppose your guy don't win?"

"We got the whole office in the bag. Don't worry. I even got some homeboys that's gonna look out for you in there."

"Next thing you know, I'm in the pen, eating baloney sandwiches and Jello."

"And did your uncle keep his word?"

"Yes. He kept his word. I was out, right after the election. But somebody used my gun, in an armored car robbery, before I went to prison. They killed the driver with my Glock."

"Let's get back to Miss Cushionberry. What happened the next time you saw her?"

"I don't know why it matters. But okay."

I didn't say anything when she walked in.

"One hour ma'am."

A slam and a clank. Heavy heels on tile for fourteen steps, and we were as alone as we could be. She had great legs - even in flat shoes. I could trace the curves of her face from memory. Her skirt fit like it loved her. I tried not to notice.

"Good morning, Mister Harris."

I was feeling a certain way about not seeing her for a month. But tough guys don't 'catch' feelings. So I answered when she asked again.

"I said good morning, Mister Harris."

I laced my fingers together, put my elbows on the table and leaned forward as far as the shackle chains would let me.

"Good morning."

She was polite.

"How've you been?"

I wasn't polite.

"Where you been? You said you'd be back on Thursday."

She sat down and stared at her watch, for long enough to make her point.

"It's Thursday."

I had to laugh.

"Good point."

She opened that leather-bound notebook of hers.

"Last time we talked about your brief stint in Jackson State Penitentiary. What I'd like to hear now, is how you went from living in your Aunt Sharon's basement, to being an enforcer for the mob in less than two months?"

"How'd you know about that?"

"I went to Detroit."

Smart lady.

"Sure. Whatever you want. We don't get much company in here."

"Mister Harris?"

"Call me Walter."

"No profanity, or I walk."

I shook my head.

"My mother had two brothers and a sister. Uncle Walter was the oldest. Aunt Sharon was the youngest. She took me in for the summer after I finished high school, and helped me get a last minute scholarship to Tuskegee University."

"Very impressive. Did you go?"

"Why is that even a question? Of course I went."

"Go on."

"I was home for the summer, between my sophomore and junior year. Aunt Sharon's husband was a doctor. They had a big new house out in Bloomfield Hills. There weren't many Black folks out there back in the day; so I was bored. But I did have one friend."

I smiled on the inside.

"Her name was…"

"Vicky Bliss."

Not only did gorgeous lawyer lady finish my sentence, but she pulled a picture of Vicky out of her notebook and slid it across the table.

"So now you all up in my personal business?"

"Mister Harris, you're a dead man walking. You don't have any business that isn't my business too."

The picture was black and white. Vicky was young and beautiful.

"She was a natural blonde, you know."

I tried my best not to be moved, but Miss Cushionberry saw right through me, and waited while I cried.

"I didn't mean to upset you Mister Harris."

"I'm not upset. It's just that..."

"What's wrong?"

"Can I call you Bonnie?"

"I'd rather not get personal..."

"You'd rather not get *personal*?"

"I'm sorry. I mean it wouldn't be..."

I just stared at her with tears in my eyes. She nodded.

"Okay, Walter. Call me Bonnie."

"I always liked that picture, Bonnie. Where'd you get it?"

"From her parents. They still live in the same house."

"You must not have told them it was for me."

"Walter." She looked me in the eye. "It was their idea. They wanted you to have it. Please, continue."

""Vicky was the only friend I had out there. Her parents put her out when they found out about us. She got a place down on Woodward, to be near her job. But she was already pregnant by then.

I met Al when I was waiting on the stairs in front of her building.

"Player, player," he said with that slick fast talkin voice. "What you doin for the cause?"

I rang the bell again, wishing she'd ring me in, so I didn't have to deal with this character.

"What cause?"

"Why *your* cause of course. I got something for ya player."

"Brother, I really don't have time for..."

Al reached in his front pocket and pulled out a wad of cash that would choke a horse.

"You ain't got time for prosperity?"

He had my attention. He pointed at my Javelin.""

"Your what?"

"My old car was an American Motors Javelin."

She finally wrote something in her notebook.

"Go on."

""Anyway, Al says, "Brother, all I need is a ride downtown."

I was just anxious to see my girl.

"Like I said man, I don't have…"

Al peeled off a crispy hundred and said:

"Money talks."

"Who is it?"

It was Vicky. I should'a went in. But that hundred was talkin loud.

"It's me, baby. But I gotta make a quick run; okay?"

"Can you bring me a Vernor's when you come back?""

Bonnie was confused, again.

"What's a Vernor's?"

"Vernor's gingerale."

"So you went with Al?"

"Yeah, but Al didn't really need a ride; he needed a sucker."

"Something ain't right, brother man. How's a ride downtown worth a hundred dollars?"

"That's a nice lil'ride I saw you get out of."

"No it's not. And I ain't down for no robberies."

"Player, player. Al ain't no criminal. Al's a hustler. Come on, I'll explain on the way."

I never trusted people that refer to themselves in third person.

"Give me the hundred first."

"Tell you what - I'm gonna tear this hundred in half…"

"Whoa, what're you doin?"

"Half now - half when you drop me off. Cool?"

"Okay, give it here."

I looked the torn bill over, front and back.

"Let's go."

Al tipped his hand when he turned his nose up at my car.

"I'm Al. I'm new around here. I just flew in from Philly, last night. My boy was supposed to pick me up and show me around, but he got shot yesterday."

"Shot?"

And he was way too familiar with a city he'd never been in before last night.

"His people told me he was gonna pull through. Lafayette is a one-way street down here, Player, so go past it and go around the block."

"I told you twice, already, my name is Mike. And why are you going to the jewelry district."

He gave me that impatient gangster stare. I guess I was supposed to be intimidated or something, but it just bounced right off me.

"I like money, Mike. Do you like money?"

"Not enough to go to jail over it."

"It ain't even like that. Turn left right here."

I had a bad feeling about Al. But half a hundred equals zero.

"I'm in the jewelry business. People love jewelry. Especially jewelry they can't afford. Make another left here."

"Look man, I don't really care. I'm just a college student, home for the summer."

"Oh, you Joe College, huh?"

His smile reminded me of a shark.

"Pull over right here, Joe College. I'll be back in a few."

"Al," I told him as he got out. "If you rob that place, I'm leaving you. I mean it."

"Aw, naw, Mike - it's not what you think. You can come in with me if you want to."

I couldn't see how that would be better, so I said:

"I'll wait."

He was in there so long, that I had time to buy Vicky's Vernor's, and call her on the pay phone. Boy, she really let me have it.

"You're downtown with who?"

"This guy named Al. He just needed a quick…"

"Philadelphia Al?"

"Yeah, that's right. I'll be back in a minute."

"No you won't. Al's a con man."

"Wait a minute. How do you know so much about Al?"

"He lives in my building. Everybody on the block knows he's a con man. You're so naïve."

"Should I leave him?"

The question was mute. Al came out of the jewelry store with a fancy bag. He wasn't smiling like a shark. And he was eating from a handful of peanuts. With a totally innocent face he said:

"Come on man," he spat out a piece of shell. "Let's go."

"I'll be there in fifteen minutes, Vicky."

I looked in his eyes for criminal intent.

"What?" He asked and cracked open a peanut.

"Nevermind; let's go."

Bonnie smiled the smile I'd expected from Al; the 'you got conned' smile.

"So, did you get the other half of the hundred?"

I had to laugh myself.

"No. I got five fake gold coins that I sold for three hundred. I was hooked after that. We did it all day - everyday. The more I made, the bolder I got. Al let me think buying that Glock was my idea."

"Come on, Mike. Let's roll to the gun store."

"Man, you got money runnin outta your ears. When you gonna buy yourself a car?"

"I already told you; I'm savin up for a Mercedes. Now come on, let's go check out some hardware."

When we got there, it was the same ole thing.

"That's a 1911 .45 right there. I got two of em back home."

"Yeah, I know. And a .357 and a Mossberg shotgun."

But I liked the Glocks.

"What you think about these, Al?"

"I don't know, Mike. They ain't got no safety. My boy back home blew his nuts off. You don't want one a those."

"The safety is in the trigger," I told him.

"Man, a good con don't need no gun."

"Then how come you drag me down here every other day."

"I just like lookin at em - that's all."

"Before I knew it, I had the big Glock 21, and a fake belly holster. Everything we did; was with my car, my gun, my ID. Al never built a life he couldn't walk away from.

Meanwhile, Vicky was five months pregnant, from us hanging out over spring break. I was either gonna have to drop out of school, or score big enough to leave her some big money. It was me who spotted the Rolls in Big Sal's shop."

Bonnie laced her fingers together, like mine, and looked at me the same way Vicky had, when she said:

"Did it ever occur to you that Al and Sal set you up?"

"I always liked that picture of Vicky. It's getting yellow now."

"Bonnie Cushionberry got you your first stay of execution with that theory, Walter. She was a very smart Lawyer."

"Yes…she was. And a Christian too. Whenever she mentioned God, it was like she knew Him personally. Do you believe in God, Doc?"

"I suppose I would - if I needed to."

"That's not an answer."

"Then no, Walter - I don't. And I think our time would be better served if we concentrate on the case."

"Please don't play the tape today, Doc. I had another one of those dreams last night. It's getting hard to tell what's real anymore."

"Okay Walter. But you have to stop fighting me. I'm on your side. And you were manipulated every step of the way. Your feelings of guilt, *and* those dreams, are the byproduct of a conscience; one that you were tricked out of using.

Hurting Miss Cushionberry didn't make things any better. Your mind is seeking a place of refuge and solace. Hence, your new wife and your little square house. But your feelings of guilt ensured that it all came crashing down on you."

"Please, Doctor Wilson. I'm trying to tell you that, *that* world seems realer than this one."

"And you'd rather live there, as a serial rapist and a murderer?"

"I don't know, Doc. I just wanna know what's real. Come on - unchain me, so I can try the 'tell."

"Isn't that how you ended up hurting Bonnie Cushionberry, Walter?"

"I didn't mean for it to happen. I guess we got too close. At some point I didn't want to talk about the case anymore. I just wanted to have a regular conversation, for once."

"When I was a kid, I wanted to be an astronaut. Weird huh?"

"I'm not your psychiatrist, Walter; I'm your lawyer. You're scheduled for execution in forty-nine days. Forty-nine days and you're in the electric chair. Forty-nine days. We need to concentrate on your stay of execution."

"Come on, Bonnie; we've been at this for a year."

"It's been two years. And you don't seem to care."

"Two years, huh? In all that time, we never had a personal conversation."

"That's not what I'm here for."

"You *see* me here, Bonnie. But you can't imagine what it's like *being* here. I live outside of time. It's always *now*. Nothing real, to remember from yesterday. Nothing to look forward to, tomorrow.

The floor is cold. The walls are cold. The food is cold. The guards are cold. I don't have a clock. Time ticks by in meals. Tick, tick, tick - that's a day. I don't have a mirror, so I can't see myself aging. I only have solace in sleep…"

"Walter, we don't have time for this. We need to…"

"I don't want to talk about the case today, Bonnie. If I only have seven more weeks to talk to a human being, I'd rather spend it having real conversations."

"Okay, Walter. So you like to sleep? I guess I understand."

"It's not the sleep, as much as it is the dreams. They gave me meds, to keep me from being depressed. What a joke. They don't want me to steal their joy by killing myself. I wouldn't take it. I think they put it in my food. It makes me have, what the prison *quack* calls lucid dreams."

"Come again?"

"Lucid dreams. As real as the reality of us sitting in this room. Realer than these chains holding me in this metal chair."

I don't think she understood what I was trying to say.

"I'll speak to the prison psychiatrist, if it bothers you."

"It used to, but not now. Those dreams give me another life. A real life outside of my cell on death row. When I go to sleep here, I wake up there - in a little square house. I have life there, Bonnie. Have you ever been married?"

She didn't say anything for a long time. I thought she wasn't going to answer. But then she put down her pen and stared off into space.

"Yes, Walter. I was married. We had a little house too. It was on a hill. My husband was a good man - gone a lot. He was a fireman."

"Did you have kids?

She looked at me and smiled.

"No. We never got a chance."

I told her I was sorry. And I meant it.

"What happened?"

"He got trapped in a fire. He didn't die right away. He rotted away, in a coma. I know what it's like to live outside of time. Time ticked when I visited him, twice a week. Sort of like now - with you."

I stopped practicing law. I just didn't see any point. It was only my faith in my friend, Jesus of Nazareth that brought me through it. Yours, was my first case since my husband died, five years before I met you. It's all I've been working on."

We sat there for a long time. I felt as sorry for her as she did for me.

"So, you wanted to be an astronaut, huh?"

And she laughed - sort of.

"I sure did. But not for the reasons you might think."

She gave me a questioning look, so I went on.

"I didn't fit in, Bonnie. I never did. Not anywhere. I started drinking when I was thirteen. I guess I never learned to socialize. I was always fascinated with space. Astronauts were my heroes.

I thought I'd volunteer for a one-way trip to a distant planet, so I wouldn't have to deal with people anymore. I thought I would grow old and die alone. Guess I got my wish."

Boy, we sure did cry that day. She took my hands to pray. That's when the guard came in to stop the visit. But I wouldn't let go of Bonnie's hands. When he pepper-sprayed me, Bonnie went into anaphylactic shock. She was allergic to pepper-spray.

I thought she'd died. The guards gave me the silent treatment, whenever I asked about her. They finally told me that I'd broken her thumb, in the scuffle. It felt like God didn't want anything to do with me.

The next time I saw her, we started off talking about Kotrin Sully. I didn't want to. But she insisted.

"Bonnie, I'm sorry about…"

"They're only giving us ten minutes, Walter. What, exactly, did Sal Manzoni say to you, when he sent you to Oklahoma City?"

I squirmed a little; trying to get comfortable. The shackles were extra tight that day. The guards knew I was enjoying Bonnie's visits. One of em looked back and forth between us, and gave the cuffs an extra squeeze.

""Well…basically he said, "I own you, punk. You'll go where I tell you.""

"And did he mention Kotrin Sully, by name?"

"No. He just told me he needed me to lean on some holdouts in his brother's protection racket."

"Did he say why he was sending *you*, specifically?"

""No. But Uncle Wack did. "Oklahoma's an electric chair state.""

Bonnie came back two days later with the petition for my appeal. I didn't want to waste our time reading it. I just signed where she told me to sign. I wanted to talk to her about my dreams. The prison shrink wasn't gonna waste his time with a dead man walking.

She asked if I'd had any good dreams, lately. So, I told her about the dream factory. She stretched her arms across the table and touched my hand.

"Are you telling me that you think I might be a *dreamgirl*?"

My heart raced, Doc. I couldn't remember the last time I'd been touched by a real woman. But I don't know if she was real. I don't know if *you're* real.

Anyway - one of the guards yelled, over the speaker.

"No contact!"

But I etched a picture of her beautiful hands, in my mind.

"I think you're real, Bonnie. I'd like to anyway. But I'm chained to this chair."

I looked down at the bolts, holding the chair to the floor.

"The only way I would know for sure, is to use the *tell*."

She gave me a weird look; like she really wanted to believe me. I didn't wait for her to ask me to explain.

"Okay, it's like this. If I can lift both feet off the ground, without falling, I know I'm dreaming."

She looked under the table, at the bolts holding the chair to the floor, and nodded. She *got* it.

"Why're you lookin' at me like that, Doc?"

"Because you're speaking in generalities. Maybe if you used more detail, you would see that the history in this reality is real. For example; you mention guards, but you never call them by name."

"Oh God. Ohhhh God."

"What's wrong, Walter?"

"The guards don't have names. No, no, no, no. Somethings wrong. The guards don't have names. None of this is real. I gotta wake up. WAKE UP."

I woke up in a cold sweat - in my little square house. Doctor Wilson's face dissolved. I'm home. There's no rape. No murder. No Sal. No Bonnie. Oh God. I'm losing it.

I laid there sweating, in a tangle of sheets and blankets. I had to wake up my wife. But I couldn't remember her name. Maybe it's Bonnie. No that's not her name. Then she rolled over.

SQUID. AHHHHHHHHH!!

"Li-shhhhh-Hou-shhhhh-Mars-shhhhh-Ac-shhhhhh. Come-shhhhh-you gotta wake up."

"Huh? Wha…"

"Little House, this is Mars Actual. Wake up, Mark!!!"

"Wait a minute. What the…"

"Little House. Come in, Little House. Key your mic, Mark. Key your mic, if you hear me.

"Mars Actual, this is Little House. Um…Am I Mark Watney?"

"Come on, man. You can't be asking that, every time you wake up. You're Mark Kent. You're not Mark Watney. You're not Matt Damon. And this is not a movie. Stand by. I'm gonna get Doctor Wilson on a head set."

"Doctor Wilson here, Mark. How're you feeling?"

"Groggy as hell, Doc. What's our status?"

"We just stirred you out of cryo. Your Dopamine and Serotonin levels are approaching normal. We commanded a little extra Epinephrine, this time, so you wouldn't wake up confused."

"How long was I out this time?"

"Forty-five days, Mark."

"It's good to be back. I been having the craziest dreams."

"It's normal. We have to keep your brain active while you're asleep. I'll command less Dopamine next time. Let's go through your bio checklist. Start with visual"

"Okay. I can see Mars out my starboard window. Red and clear. My control panel is crisp. Telemetry is live and counting. Is Bonnie up? Hey Bonnie, you up?"

"How do you read me, Mark.?"

"Five by five, Doc. Loud and clear. Are me and Bonnie ever gonna be on the same sleep schedule?"

"Don't worry about Major Cushionberry right now. Let's check your mental acuity. Count backwards, by threes - starting from a hundred."

"One hundred, ninety-seven, ninety-four, ninety-one, eighty-eight, eighty-five. Doc?"

"Keep counting, Mark."

"Eighty-two, seventy-nine, seventy-six, seventy-three."

"That's fine mark. Check your intravenous food supply, please."

"Thirty-nine percent left in this canister. Two canisters left. Is that enough to make it home? I'm gonna check Bonnie's."

"Mark! Don't!"

"Hey Doc? How's it possible that Bonnie has seven full canisters? What are you doing; starving her?"

"Shhhhhhhhhhhhhhh…"

"Hey guy's. I can't hear you. Come in, Mars Actual."

"Shhhhhhhhh…Mark?"

"Okay, I can hear you now."

"Mark… Major Cushionberry died over a year ago. Don't you re-member?"

General Bonnie Cushionberry lie, inclined, on an operating table in Bethesda Maryland, surrounded by the navy's finest neural-surgical team. Below her forehead, her face was wrapped in gauze. Below her neck, her body was covered with a cryo-cooled blanket. Bonnie's boney skull cap sat soaking in a vat of bio-gel, made from her own DNA. The same gel covered her exposed brain.

"Standby, one, Mark."

Doctor Harvey Wilson, dressed in a white Surgical Protection and Concealed Environment (SPACE) suit, motioned to a technician in the observation booth, overlooking the operating room. The tech turned up the background static generator that kept Mark from hearing the doctors confer; through Bonnie's ears.

Doctor Wilson switched his audio from the operating room to the booth,

"So, what do I tell him?" He asked the ever-growing team of subject matter experts in the booth.

Most shrugged, but a uniformed and highly decorated Air Force Colonel answered.

"You're the only Neural Psychiatric Detective in the country, as far as I know. Tell him what he needs to hear."

Doctor Wilson was a tall man; head and shoulders taller than anyone else in the room. When he walked to the elevated booth, he was almost eye-to-eye with a seated Colonel Gillis.

"And *that* is precisely the problem, colonel. And the very reason that you're here. This *man* is not a man. He is a construct of General Cushionberry's thalamic reticular activation system."

"In English, Doctor. We all know he's not a man."

"Mark Kent is a neural predator; escaped from the general's dream factory. He has access to all her sensory and intellectual memory. And he's gobbling up more neural real estate, by the hour. We're all tired. We've been chasing him all night, while you slept and showered and…"

The lead surgeon, Doctor Kotrin Sully, scolded him.

"I will have decorum in my operating room, Doctor Wilson. I have half the patient's skull cut open. Get on with it."

"My apologies." Doctor Wilson went on. "That array of micro-antennas around her head, are tracking the physical whereabouts of the predator. We have to trap him in his own reality. General Cushionberry is the commander of NORAD Space Command. He's smart - as smart as she is. I'm just a psychiatrist.

We need a story he'll believe, so he'll stay put. So far, he's dodged us at every turn; flickering between realities. The last time we were *here*, he said he was in *Mars tow*. No one here knew what it meant. So, we put the General in a coma, until *you* arrived.

Colonel Peter 'Dobie' Gillis, a friend of Bonnie's, and commander of one of the satellite ground stations under the General's command, furrowed his brow.
"What happens when you trap him?"

Doctor Sully pointed to the business ends of three suitcase-sized, white, conformal coated packages, suspended above the General's exposed brain. A conical metal barrel pointed at Bonnie's head, from each package, just below the radiation warning symbols.
"We're going to cauterize him, with converging neutron beams."

Colonel Gillis nodded.
"What about the General? Will it harm her?"
Doctor Wilson answered, "Not if we separate their neural networks. We have to get her off his mind, so to speak. And, Colonel…"
"Yeah?"
"We need him trapped in a circumstance where he expects to be in searing pain."
"And he thinks he's on a spaceship near Mars?"

Doctor Wilson nodded.
"That's right. His call sign is 'Little House.'"
"Will it give us away, if he hears my voice?"
Doctor Wilson pondered for a moment, and concluded;
"A familiar voice? It might actually help. Let's just use a different name, to keep the General out of the conversation."

"**L**ittle House, this is Mars Actual."

The answer came from Bonnie Cushionberry's lips.

"Little House, here. I'm a little confused, Doc. I can hardly tell what's real anymore."

"It's okay, Mark. I'm gonna put you on with flight ops."

Doctor Wilson nodded to the observation booth, where Colonel Gillis wore a headset.

"Hey ole buddy. Colonel Grissom here. How ya doin out there?"

"Say again?"

"It's Colonel Grissom, Mark. Flight Ops. Let's go over the flight plan. Doctor Wilson wants to know how much you remember."

"Forgive my skepticism, colonel. Do you have a first name?"

"Shhhhhhhhhh."

"Mars Actual. Little House. You're fading. Do you read?"

"Shhhhhhhh - Mars Actual, here. It's me, Mark - Dobie. Let's get on with it. How much do you remember about your mission?"

"I don't remember Major Cushionberry dying. That's for damn sure. I'm gonna go check on her…"

"Belay that, Mark - shhhhhhhhhhhhhh - you're coming up on a critical burn. We need you to concentrate. You *do* know how you ended up in *Mars tow?*"

"Yeah, Dobie. We missed a critical burn. We're chasing Mars around the sun. We'll never catch up…unless."

"Unless what, Mark."

"Unless we reverse thrust and spiral into an orbit closer to the sun."

"That's right Mark. The classic Hohman transfer. Shhhhhhh. Shhhhhhh. Shhhhhhh. We've already run the numbers on that maneuver, Mark. You and I both know it would still take years to catch up to Mars. The earth will catch up faster than that."

"Copy that. Are you suggesting we wait for the next earth transfer window?"

"Shhhhhhhhhhhhhhhhhh. Negative on earth transfer. We have a better plan. We've calculated a trajectory toward the sun. The sun's gravity will get you up to 67,000 mph, relative to…"

"You wanna slingshot me around the sun to catch up with Mars?"

"Negative, Mark. We want you to take Bonnie's body home to earth. Shhhhhhh."

Doctor Wilson applauded, silently.

"Well done, colonel."

Colonel Gillis adjusted his tie and leaned forward.

"Will he go for it? The general can do the math, on the fly."

"Not in her sleep, she can't. Dreams are a *right* brain phenomenon. Math is done with our *left* hemisphere. Talk him through the burn, and we'll put her back in a coma. When we bring her back to dream-state, you'll convince him that he's headed directly into the sun."

"I can do that." The colonel answered. "Somebody bring me something to write with. And some strong black coffee."

One of Doctor Wilson's protégés handed the colonel a notebook and pen. Doctor Wilson waited while Colonel Gillis scribbled something in the notebook. At the colonel's 'thumb up', Doctor Wilson cued the tech.

"Little House, this is Mars Actual."

"Go ahead, Dobie." Came from Mark, in Bonnies voice."

"Mark, your burn profile has been uploaded. Verify telemetry please."

"Mars Actual, my vision is getting a little blurry. I see numbers changing, but I can't be sure that..."

"Don't worry about it, Mark. We'll loop your telemetry back to Mars Actual. Standby one,"

Colonel Gillis paused for effect.

"Little House. Mars Actual. Your telemetry is good. Your Apogee Kick Motor is gonna burn for two minutes, fourteen seconds. That's a lot of G's, Mark. Expect to pass out."

"Copy, Mars Actual. But when I come to, we're gonna talk about Major Cushionberry."

"Anything you say, Mark. Coming up on one minute, and counting."

"Mars Actual; what about the checklist?"

"No time, Mark. It's now or never. Thirty seconds. Hold on tight. There'll be a four 'G' punch in your back. On my mark - in ten, nine, eight, seven. All systems go. Five, four, three, two, one, fire."

Doctor Wilson motioned to the anesthesiologist and mouthed words through the glass in his SPACE helmet.

"Put her out."

D octor Wilson un-donned his SPACE suit and met his team of psychiatrists and subject matter experts in the fourth-floor conference room, where dossiers lie spread out on a large mahogany table.

"Okay, let's make sure we're all up to speed."

He made introductions, starting with Colonel Gillis.

"For those of you who haven't met him, this is Colonel Peter 'Dobie' Gillis. He's known the general since the Air Force Academy. Going around the room:

- My protégé's; Doctors Atworth and Kataria.
- Vicky Harris; for family references. She's General Cushionberry's daughter-in-law. Her husband, Michael, is doing ten years in Oklahoma, for racketeering.
- Deputy sheriffs Finnegan and Reese. They've both been prison guards.
- Air Force Nurse William Cox here, is the voice of the base on Mars. He's apparently seen the movie, 'The Martian', as many times as the general."

That drew a few snickers, to which Colonel Gillis commented,

"This is no laughing matter. General Cushionberry is...was the head of NORAD Space Command; responsible for defending the U.S. against any weapon entering our airspace from above..."

He caught himself.

"Above a classified altitude. And you're about to lobotomize that asset."

"It's not a lobotomy, colonel," Doctor Wilson corrected. "It's a cutting-edge precision microscopic…"

"Finish the introductions, doctor!" The colonel snapped.

"Continuing around the room:

- Senator Dayton; Homeland Security.
- Senator Hughes; Senate Armed Services Committee.

And who are you?"

"Rachael Johnson; chief hospital administrator."

Senator Dayton challenged her.

"Are you cleared?"

Rachael shot back, flashing the badge that the senator obviously didn't see.

"This is *my* hospital. You're damned right I'm cleared. And your cutting-edge procedure is costing the tax payers forty-two million dollars. Skip the introductions and get on with it."

Doctor Wilson went on.

"The gelatinous compound that's protecting the general's brain has a useful half-life of just over thirteen hours. We started last night, because of the drain on resources. Doctor Sully is going to close her up at noon. That gives us less than three hours to incapacitate the predator.

The micro antenna array is reading micro-volts, as it is. Nothing will register, once the general's skullcap has been replaced. We can't afford anymore wrinkles in the continuity of the predator's dreamscape."

Senator Hughes had been nervously drumming a pen.

"Doctor Wilson, the president is in Strategic Arms negotiations with the Russians. The general's input is critical. How do we know the general's condition is not the result of some bio-weapon?"

Senator Dayton, the senate minority whip argued to the contrary.

"That would be all too bizarre. It would have been easier for them to eliminate her from the equation."

Colonel Gillis settled the matter.

"Respectfully, Senator Dayton - she *has* been removed from the situation."

Doctor Wilson took back the floor.

"Let's go over what we've gleaned so far. The predator is dithering between three highly entrenched realities. In all three, we're coaxing him towards a fiery end. If he expects it, he'll stay put while we cauterize the billion-or-so neurons that make up his consciousness.

In the first reality, he's evolved into a serial rapist and a murderer. He's moved through a lot of neural-matter since we first got him talking. There's a college campus; Tuskegee, we think."

The colonel nodded, and added,

"She graduated top of her class."

Doctor Wilson pointed to two women and two men sitting at the far end of the confer.

"I didn't get a chance to introduce our research team. They've gathered the background material and pictures you see on the table. There's Tuskegee University, circa nineteen seventy-five.

He also talked about a place called 'Midtown', with a big assembly plant and a junior college. Any ideas?"

The researchers mumbled amongst themselves. But it was Vicky that raised her hand.

"Do you have something, Mrs. Harris?"

"I don't know why I didn't think of it before. Bonnie's grandparents, on her mother's side, lived in Middleton, Oklahoma."

The researchers tapped and scrolled on notebook computers.

"Got it." One of the women announced. "Middleton, Oklahoma. Population 37,000. There used to be a Ford Truck chassis assembly plant there. It closed its doors in nineteen eighty-one."

The other woman added,

"Middleton Junior College is still there…"

One of the men jumped her track.

"A string of rapes there in seventy-four."

Doctor Wilson beamed.

"That probably gets us to O…"

The final researcher was ahead of him.

"Oklahoma City is sixty-two miles from Middleton."

Several in the room over-talked each other; conjecturing about grisly murders. One of the sheriffs steered the debate to Oklahoma State Penitentiary's electric chair.

"Old Sparky. Frying brains since nineteen fifteen."

Colonel Gillis had heard enough banter. He pounded the table with an iron fist.

"That woman lying in there with her brain exposed is my friend. I hear one more joke, and as God is my witness, I'm going to put one of you to sleep. Move on, Doctor Wilson."

Doctor Wilson nodded in agreement.

"Both the first two scenarios end up on Oklahoma State Penitentiary's death row. Any insights?"

"He mentioned seventeen steps to his cell," Vicky offered. "Is that important?"

The remote printer whined, from the far corner, printing pictures that streamed from the researchers' notebooks.

"It was fourteen steps. And it wouldn't be to his cell."

Doctor Wilson pointed to a stack of stapled handouts, in front of the research team. One of the research men whispered,

"Transcripts. Pass them around," as the sheriff went on.

"It's an interrogation cell with a metal chair bolted to the floor. There'll be a priest, and a last meal, before the executioners come for him."

"Make it a pastor." Colonel Gillis specified. "The general's a Christian."

Rachael pushed her chair back and headed for the door, phone in hand.

"I'll call in a chaplain, just in case."

She stepped out to make the call, standing just outside the open door.

Doctors Atworth and Kataria leaned toward each other whispering. Then Doctor Kataria spoke softly, with an Indian accent.

"We need to address his *tell*, Harvey. Every time he mentions it, the general moves her feet."

Doctor Atworth elaborated.

"It works because there's no gravity in the dreamer's vertical axis."

Doctor Atworth must've seen confusion in the conferee's faces. He mocked sleep, laying his head sideways on praying hands.

"The dreamer is sleeping horizontally, you see. If we could trick her brain into believing there is gravity under her feet; well then…"

He didn't finish his sentence.

"And just how do you propose we do that?" Senator Hughes asked.

The room fell silent…until Rachael leaned her head in the door.

"Bump the operating table, beneath her feet. It won't budge, but she'll feel it."

Eyebrows raised, on nodding heads, when Rachael leaned back out of the doorway.

A Black, Navy Seaman sat, wearily nodding off, in a chair against the conference room wall.

"Seaman Ross over there…"

And Ross answered dutifully, after hearing Doctor Wilson mention his name.

"Sir. Yes, sir. Sorry, sir."

"It's okay, son. Seaman Brady Ross is from Detroit. We used his, and Sheriff Finnegan's voices to make the recording I've been playing back in the second scenario. He's also helping us - him and Vicky, with the geography of Detroit city. Most of us have been up all night. All of you, read over the transcripts. We need to trap him in a scenario he believes is real. And we don't have much time."

Rachael came in finishing her phone conversation and closing the conference room door.

"…And coffee for twelve – STAT!"

The view from behind the surgical barrier looked like something out of a Frankenstein movie. The front two thirds of General Cushionberry's head was open to the surgical stage. Cool fluorescent spotlights shined through spaces in the parabolic net of micro-voltaic antenna sensors suspended above her head, revealing gelatinous goo that protected her brain from contamination. IV tubes protruded like electrodes and wires from her neck.

A SPACE suited surgical team stood behind trays of instruments, in case an intrusive operation became necessary. The non-intrusive team manned keyboards and screens the controlled sensors and neutron guns. A three-dimensional hologram of Bonnie's brain floated just above her forehead.

A freshly scrubbed and SPACE suited Dr. Sully came in, after the hiss of the airlock door, and took center stage.

"Listen up team," he announced; his voiced slightly muffled by the filter baffles in his SPACE suit. We have less than two hours before I'll be forced, by the nature of the DNA gel, to close the general's skull. The gel is already starting to disintegrate. I don't need to remind any of you that this surgery is a matter of national security. Doctor Wilson."

"Thank you, Kotrin. Because this is a non-invasive procedure, so to speak, we are hopeful that we can have the general back on her feet, as soon as her skull begins to knit.

We need this neural parasite, isolated from the general's consciousness and clear of blood vessels. Our targeting system will tell us when he's distant, stationary, and safe to fire upon. Eight minutes - that's how long we need him stationary. He'll only stay put if he believes he has no other option.

You've read the transcripts. You've been briefed on the backgrounds of the patient and the predator. No one is to speak, unless directed by me. We'll have to meet him in any of the three most probable scenarios he'll wake up in. Charge the neutron guns."

Heavy relays flipped in the conformal coated packages.
    'Ka-thunk, ka-thunk, ka-thunk.'
    "Bring up the antenna array. One microvolt sensitivity."
    A tech typed on one of many keyboards.
    "Array active - at one microvolt."

Doctor Wilson nodded.
    "Engage tracking."
    Servo motors whirred and spun up, increasing in pitch until they became inaudible.
    "Ok, let's bring them up to dream-state one. Serotonin, to baseline. Dopamine to D.S. one."
    Harvey looked around.
    "Everybody quiet. Epinephrine, to Lucid, plus ten percent."

They all waited, while the endorphins took effect. Eventually, the general's body twitched.
    "Doctor Wilson?"
    "I'm here."
    "Where am I?"

Doctor Wilson stalled; not knowing which scenario they were in. The cryo-blanket moved as the general shifted underneath.

Testing the restraints? Harvey guessed they were in scenario one or two. But the dreamer in scenario one remained unnamed, so he didn't use one.

"Are the handcuffs too tight?"

"I can't see, Harvey. Is it over?"

Oh God. She's awake.

The people in the observation booth bristled at the realization.

"Bonnie?"

"Is it over? Did it work?"

"Major Cushionberry? Mars Actual told me you were dead."

"Who's that, Harvey?"

"They can't hear you, Bonnie. We're on a trajectory toward the sun."

Doctor Wilson stood speechless as the patient and predator both used the general's vocal cords. *They're talking to each other.*

"I'm confused, Harvey. What's going on?"

"They can't hear us, Bonnie. We're no longer in Mars tow. We're gonna slingshot around the sun. We're going home."

Doctor Wilson crossed figurative fingers, hoping the general would catch on. He had the distinct impression that he was listening to two different people. Everybody, in and out of the booth, exchanged questioning glances.

"Do you copy, Bonnie? We're going home."

"Copy that, shipmate. What's our status?"

Spectators stood in awe, as General Bonnie Cushionberry took command. Doctor Wilson eased toward the cryo-blanket console and set the temperature for a fast ramp to a hundred degrees. He typed the word's, >SHE KNOWS>, on a common screen, for all to see.

"I say again. What's are status?"

"Come on, Bonnie. We've been stuck in this tin can together for two years. Call me Mark."

Beads of sweat formed on the general's forehead.

"Do you feel that, Mark? The hull is overheating. I'm checking our trajectory. Standby one."

"Copy that, Bonnie."

Minutes went by. Doctor Wilson typed at a keyboard, to four common screens; three in the O.R. and one in the booth. >SHE'S STALLING. WE"RE TARGETING>.

"Mark?"

"Yeah, Bonnie."

"We're coming in too steep."

"I know. It's getting awful hot."

A three-dimensional, red curser lit up in the hologram."

Doctor Wilson waited for >TARGET AQUIRED> to scroll across his screen, and inched his hand toward the 'ARM' switch. He flipped it, and >TARGET LOCKED> scrolled across his screen.

>TARGET LOCKED> scrolled across the common screens. Doctor Wilson was just about to press the flashing, green 'FIRE' button. The general stayed perfectly in character, all the way till the end.

"We're entering the solar corona, Mark. It'll all be over soon."

But someone sneezed, while she was talking. The 'FIRE' button stopped flashing. >TARGET LOST> scrolled across the common screens. Doctor Wilson's eyes widened as he pointed the culprit to the airlock door. But it was too late. The predator jumped to another scenario, in a different location.

"Damn guards. They can't give us one minute of privacy?"

Doctor Wilson took the lead; guessing they were in scenario two.

"It's too late, Walter. The governor denied your stay of execution. Bonnie came to see you before…well. She can't go in with you."

Harvey shot a pointing finger at the chaplain in the booth.

"Walter, I'm Pastor Jenkins. I'm here to read you your last rights.

The LORD *is* my shepherd;
I shall not want.
He makes me to lie down in green pastures;
He leads me beside the still waters.
He restores my soul;
He leads me in the paths of righteousness

For His name's sake.
Yea, though I walk through the valley of the shadow of death,
I will fear no evil;
For You *are* with me;
Your rod and Your staff, they comfort me.
You prepare a table before me in the presence of my enemies;
You anoint my head with oil;
My cup runs over.
Surely goodness and mercy shall follow me
All the days of my life;
And I will dwell in the house of the Lord
Forever.

Doctor Wilson pointed at Sheriff Finnegan.
"Come on, Walter. It's time."
"No, no...not yet. I'll use the *tell* and you'll all disappear."

Harvey Wilson bumped the table, when the general's feet twitched; hoping Bonnie knew not to interrupt.

It worked.
"Oh God, it's real."
"Come on, Walter. Just twenty-two more steps."
>TARGET AQUIRED> scrolled on the common screens.
"Don't struggle. Just sit down."
"Please, I just wanna go home to my little house."

The predator had jumped to scenario one. But >TARGET LOCKED> was scrolling and the 'FIRE' button was flashing green.
He's still in the chair. We're fine as long as he doesn't call him...

"Try to relax, Walter."

"Walter? Who's Walter? You might think you're in control, but you're just a character from the dream factory. I'm flying through that wall, and there's nothing you can do about it."

At >TARGET LOST>, Doctor Sully shook his head, and motioned for his team to prepare for closure. Doctor Wilson's disappointment turned to shock, when Colonel Gillis yelled:

"Listen to me, you son of a bitch. That brain you're screwing with doesn't belong to you. You're a neural predator - independent and autonomous. Your neural network is inside the brain of General Bonnie Cushionberry. *You* have to die, to save her. Now get back in that goddamned electric chair.

Bonnie, if you can hear me, we need you to not be here. Go and figure the Hohman Transfer formula for the Genie Mission."

"Okay, okay. Oh God, is it going to hurt?"
TARGET AQUIRED>>>TARGET LOCKED>>>
"Not for long."
FIRING>>>FIRING>>>FIRING>>>...

The general screamed.
FIRING>>>TRACKING MINOR MOTION>>>FIRING>>> FIRING...

Eventually she stopped.
>PROCEDURE COMPLETE>.

Doctor Wilson gave a thumb up. Cheers came from all around. Doctor Wilson saluted Doctor Sully.
"Close her up, Kotrin."

Harvey Wilson and Bonnie Cushionberry sat face to face, in worn leather chairs, in the doctor's not so neat office. No one spoke for a time. Bonnie stared at Harvey. Harvey stared out the window.

"How long has it been now, Bonnie?"

"Almost six months. Please look at me."

A keloid scar stretched across Bonnie's forehead, just below her hairline.

"Your incision is healing nicely."

Bile rose in Bonnie's gut. She pursed her lips to contain her anger.

"What were you thinking, Harvey?"

Harvey's eyes met Bonnie's - but only for a moment.

"I was hoping to cure you. You'll never understand, because you can't remember your condition."

"So it's a rather circular argument, isn't it? But you cut open the top of my head. And I...I just want you to tell me why you thought that was necessary?"

"It *did* work, Bonnie. I got the predator out of your head."

Bonnie leaned in, so Harvey couldn't ignore her.

"I have nightmares, Harvey. Nightmares of you standing over me, as if you were enjoying it all. I can still hear you talking to someone who wasn't there."

Harvey looked at Bonnie. But he was detached; as if he didn't understand why she was angry.

"But he *was* there, Bonnie. You spoke to him yourself, when you woke up."

"Only so you'd stop. But you didn't, did you?"

"It was for your own good."

"Oh, it was for my own good, was it? I trusted you. I let you in. I saw you for months, before you did this to me."

"It was for the good of the nation. The president needed you."

"Don't give me anymore of your bull! What you did was wrong - period!"

A hospital orderly opened the Doctor's door.

"Is everything alright, doctor?"

"Well, Bonnie?" Harvey asked. "Can you calm down?"

Bonnie composed herself - enough to get rid of the orderly.

"Sorry. I'm fine."

The orderly closed the door.

Bonnie was close enough to spit in Harvey's face. She wanted to.

"I'm going to have another plastic surgery, next week. I just wanted you to see what you did to me. And there are scars inside my head that no one will ever see. Don't you have anything to say? Don't you feel anything?"

"I tasted a donut."

"What?"

"You tried to take it from me."

"A donut? That was my *lunch*."

"It was the first time I ever tasted anything in a dream."

"It wasn't a dream, you bastard. You were wide awake!"

"You tried to take the donut. I hit you with something."

"That's right, Harvey. You hit me with my award from the Surgeon General. You knocked me out. You could've called for help. We could've gotten past that. You didn't have to mutilate me."

"We had to operate. You were dying. There was no other way. My restraints are too tight. Can you loosen them please?"

Bonnie couldn't contain herself. She spat in his face.
"I wish I'd died, you piece of crap. So you'd get the chair."

The orderly opened the door.
"Doctor Cushionberry? The guards are here to…"
"In a minute, Al."

Harvey twisted in his chair.
"I'm already doing life without the possibility of parole. Isn't that enough?"

Bonnie snatched off her wig, and threw it at him. It caught on one of the buckles, on Harvey's straight jacket, and hung there.
"You scalped me, you bastard! Look at it! Look what you did to me! You carved at my skull, with broken glass, while I begged and screamed!"
"I saved you, Bonnie. Can't you see I saved you?"

Bonnie stood up, with checkerboard scars and patches of hair on her mutilated scalp, she leaned over her patient and whispered,
"I'm going to adjust your endorphins, Harvey. You'll rarely sleep. And when you do, I pray you get lost in a never-ending nightmare."

Harvey just stared out the window. The slightest of smiles washed over his face.

Bonnie never liked working in a prison. But she gave her patients the same care and compassion she had at her former practice. She'd even let Walter watch movies. She lost the practice when her husband died in a fire. Now this - hacked up by Harvey Wilson; a deranged maniac, lost in his dreams.

"Guards! Take this scum back to the psych wing. Remove all the amenities from his cell. No more movies. No books, except for a Bible. And make sure he has nothing to write with."

This was Bonnie's first day at work, since the attack. And as they dragged Harvey away, shouting about his *tell*, she slid her name plate back into the slot, under the words:

OKLAHOMA STATE PENETENTIARY
CHIEF PSYCHIATRIST

Deranged: The End

The Soul
Catcher

Michael Kent

THE SOUL CATCHER: CHAPTER 1

It smelled like rain that day - and cool for an August morning. An old Indian Brave rose from the breakfast table and prepared to take his great-grandson out for a hike in the Arizona outback.

"Be careful out there, Babe," his fair skinned daughter-in-law warned. "And come back before it rains."

The boy, wearing jeans with an 'Angels' tee shirt, wiped steel-cut oatmeal from his chin.

"Is your name really Babe?"

The old man with two grey ponytails wore buckskin trousers and a colorful poncho.

"It sure is."

"What kind of name is that for an old man?"

"Hunter! Don't be rude," the middle-aged woman told her grandson, as she cleared away the dishes.

"Leave the boy alone, Lucy. You asked the same thing, when you met me."

The old man reached for the screen door handle - but it wasn't there.

"Who left this open?"

"You did, Babe," Lucy answered.

"Not likely."

"Dad," Lucy said, referring to Babe. "You were just out there - remember?"

Babe felt for the boy's hand.

"She calls me that when she's angry," he whispered.

Then he raised his voice to his daughter in law, Lucy.

"Remind me to close it next time."

Hunter took the old man's hand and led him out on the porch.

"You're my great grandpa, aren't you?"

Babe picked up his six foot, crooked wooden staff from beside the door.

"That's right."

"So what should I call you?"

"Call me Babe, like all the other youngins have been doing, since I first had youngins."

Hunter helped Babe down the creaky wooden stairs. His staff tapped the steps on the way down.

"This way," the old man pointed as he walked. "You like baseball?"

"Heck yeah. I'm a pitcher. I struck out three boys last week."

"Is *that* right? Who's your favorite team?"

"Angels all the way, Babe. Oh I get it. Are you named after Babe Ruth?"

"Yep. Sure am."

"Well it's a cool name, in that case. Where're we going?"

"Same place I took your father, before he died."

"I don't remember him," the boy admitted, without much emotion in his voice.

"I know," Babe said and gave the boy's hand a squeeze. "I took his father there too."

"Now *Grandpa, John,* I remember. He was your son -right?"

"You're a smart boy. You figure right."

Hunter felt sadness for the old man.

"Sorry he died," he said with a sniff.

"Are you twelve yet?"

"Not yet. But I'm almost eleven."

"We're going up to the top of this dirt road. You up for a climb?"

Hunter answered with confidence, "Yep. Just lead the way, Babe"

Babe stopped half way up the road and leaned on his staff to catch his breath.

"I haven't been up here, since I went blind. You'll have to help me."

A slightly less confident Hunter answered:

"Okay…I think."

"I hear you like rocks?"

"That's right. I got lots of em."

Babe straightened up and continued up the steep road.

"Got any red ones?"

"Yeah…well there not really red. They're kind of like burgundy."

Babe tapped his way to the top of the hill.

"Tell me what you see."

"Wow; I see everything. Look at those mountains. They're so red… Oh sorry."

"It's okay son. I see them through your eyes. Can you see a big tree?"

"I sure can. Man - it must be as old as you."

Babe's voice grew solemn.

"That's a Pinon Pine. I'm eighty years old, and that tree was here when my great grandfather brought his son up here. Think you can lead me to it?"

"I sure can."

Babe laid his staff on the ground and held up one end.

"Take the other end of my stick."

Hunter picked up the other end.

"Come on let's go."

"Make sure you don't catch your pants on those…"

"Ouch!"

"Catclaws."

Hunter weaved his way through the brush. Babe paced the six foot length of his staff, and turned where Hunter turned, a staff length ahead.

"Watch out for snake holes."

The staff stopped.

"Snake holes? Let's go back."

Babe laughed.

"They won't bother us if you steer clear of the holes. How far is the tree?"

"Home plate to second base - get it?"

"I Get it."

"I thinks it's gonna rain, Babe."

"Yeah, I smell it. We'll be back before then."

"Hey there's a porcupine."

"Stay away from him too. What else do you see?"

The staff stopped again.

"Wait. I think it's a deer. Whoa look at him go."

"Is he coming this way?"

"No."

"Run!"

"What?"

Babe snatched the staff from Hunter's grip.

"Run to the tree. Run."

"There's a wolf chasing him," Hunter called out as he lit for the big tree.

Babe tapped along the ground and hurried toward Hunter's voice.

"Run as fast as you can, boy."

The animal broke off the chase and howled, just as Hunter reached the big pine.

"I made it," he shouted. "It's okay; the deer got away."

Babe knew what the boy didn't.

"Climb!" He shouted. "Climb high!"

The old man, long past his days of running, made slow progress.

"Is it coming yet?"

"No. It's just layin there. Can I come down now?"

"No. Keep climbing."

The wolf, Babe thought, would catch his breath soon. It didn't howl like a pup. Either it was old or sick. A healthy wolf in its prime would have caught the deer.

"Uh oh; he's coming."

"How fast?"

"He's just walking, but you better hurry."

The old man picked up his pace, snagging catclaws in his pants. They hooked into his skin, like fish hooks, as he pulled away.

"How far to the tree?"

"Pitcher's mound, but you better...RUN!"

Babe not wanting to trip and fall, turned to face the wolf on his own terms.

"What are you doing, Babe? Come on, you can make it."

Ears to the wolf, Babe waited for the snarl that would come before the charge. The wolf slowed and snarled, testing the target. The old man kicked the bottom of the pine branch into a propeller spin, like he'd learned from his father. If he caught the wolf in the snout with that green pine, he could change its mind about this meal.

The growl inched closer. Babe's arthritic wrists tired quickly as he spun the staff; its ends alternating toward the animal. Hearing charging footfalls, he braced his legs for the attack. Sharp teeth pierced his buckskins, at the ankle, and snatched him off his feet.

The beast clamped down and snatched Babe one way and then the other. Pain shot through Babe's body like sharp nails. It took razor sharp focus for Babe to remain silent. He didn't dare scream. He didn't want to signal fear. But it was about to taste blood. And ravenous frenzy would follow.

Hunter looked on frozen in terror as the wolf-like creature dragged Babe. It would be just a matter of time before...

Then, surprisingly, the old man rolled on his back and gripped the staff in the middle with both hands. Whack! The right side of the staff caught the wolf behind the eye. Whack, whack - one to the opposite jaw and then back to the other shoulder.

The wolf staggered backward and fell over.

"He's down Babe. Get up."

The old Indian staggered to his feet and limped toward the tree, using his staff for a crutch.

"Come on," the boy yelled. "Follow my voice."

The monster of a wolf rolled around and found its footing. Hunter, not wanting to watch, turned his head. *What are these?* He reached for a hard, spring Pinon pine cone. He plucked it, and felt the size and weight. *A baseball.*

Hunter balanced on two big branches and wound up for the pitch, just as the wolf circled, exposing its flank. Hunter let loose a fastball that struck the wolf in the side and sounded off with a thud. The animal was clearly shaken. Thunder rumbled in the distance.

"Come on, Babe. I got you."

The little league pitcher plucked another pine cone. This time he aimed for the head and beaned the wolf right in the snout. The wolf yelped and backed off.

"Reach me your stick," the boy said when his great-grandfather made it to the tree.

Hunter reached down and helped him up to the two big branches.

The old man settled in the fork of the branches - exhaled and drew in a long breath.

"I heard what you did," he told the boy. "You're a Brave."

The wolf circled at a distance as heavy raindrops began to fall.

Babe rested in the downpour. But only for a few minutes. A lightning bolt ripped the sky, followed a second later by a thunderclap that rattled the tree. The smell of ozone filled the air.

"We can't stay here!" Babe yelled over the driving rain. "The lightning is coming this way."

"What about the wolf?" The boy yelled back over the roar of rain.

"Don't worry about him. He knows not to be near this tree in a lightning storm."

"You sure know a lot about wolves!" Hunter shouted. "He's running away."

The elder tossed his staff, and thinking he remembered the distance to the ground, he jumped. But remembering is not the same as seeing. The ground came bone-jarringly quick. Were it not for the mud, he'd have broken a leg. The boy landed beside him and helped him up.

"Come on, Great-grandpa. I'll guide you back to the house."

"Great-grandpa is it now? That means you're serious."

"Right. Let's go."

"The cliffs are closer. We'll take shelter there, and be home by lunch time."

The rain slacked, enough so they didn't have to yell.

"You're blind. The house is closer," the boy insisted.

Babe, determined to finish what he'd started, replied:

"We're not going home. Not yet."

"*I* am," Hunter told him.

"You listen to me, Hunter Strongbow…"

"It's Strong - Hunter Strong."

Babe knelt down and tapped his own chest.

"Put your hand here, over my heart."

When the younger complied, the elder put his palm over the boy's heart.

"You feel that?"

"Yes, sir."

"That's a Strongbow heart beating in your chest. Strongbow hearts are always brave. Get it?"

"I get it."

"Now guide me to the cliff, before our brave asses get struck by lightning."

The rain came back with a vengeance, and just as they reached the shelter of an overhang, lightning struck the tree with a loud crack, splitting off an upper branch. The boy scooted closer to the old man, where he felt safer.

"How do you know so much about everything, Babe?"

"My ancestors taught me. They're going to teach you too."

"Um…what does that mean?"

"Which part; ancestors, or teach you too?"

"The second part."

"I'm taking you to the 'Soul Catcher.'"

A chill shot down Hunter's spine. He didn't feel so brave.

"Soul Catcher? Who's that?"

"It's not a who. Come on - I remember the way. We'll play follow the leader."

Hunter followed Babe up an easy incline, still under the ledge. They rounded the bend, into a crevasse, in the pouring rain. Still the boy followed. Water ran ankle high, but the wide footing was etched like steps.

Babe turned his head toward the boy.

"Put your hands and feet exactly where I put mine."

"Okay Babe, I'm right behind you."

Monsoon force winds whipped rain sideways. Trapped a on mountain ledge in a deluge, with nothing between him and death, but an elderly blind man,

Hunter felt far out of his Anaheim California comfort zone. Nothing in his life had prepared him for anything like this. He thought his heart would pound out of his chest. But he trusted this old man, who blindly stood his ground against a hungry wolf.

Back against the mountain. Left foot there. Left hand in that crack. Right foot crosses left. Turn and face the mountain.

Babe switched his staff from his right hand to his left and felt for a jagged protrusion.

"Are you with me, boy?"

"Yeah, Babe. I'm right here."

"Are you scared?"

"Yes."

"Nothing wrong with being afraid. I was afraid the first time too. Just take it slow. One step, one hand, one breath at a time."

Hunter glanced down, thinking; *We're gonna die.*

"And whatever you do," Babe warned. "Don't look down."

The rain stopped, just as the sun came out over the mountain, making for an easier climb.

"Wait, Babe."

"Why? What's wrong?"

"The ledge is broken."

Hunter watched Babe reach out with his staff. The ledge was broken for about two feet.

"Hold my stick."

Babe found a hand hold and stepped across.

"It's too high," Hunter called, "I can't reach it."

"Here," Babe stretched out his left hand, while holding onto the crack, above with his right."

He grabbed the boy's hand, and took his weight.

"Careful. I got you. Don't drop my…"

"Oops. Sorry Babe."

The staff clattered to the rock below. Babe pulled Hunter across the void.

"No big deal. We'll get it on the way back down."

"Hey. I see bunnies."

"Down in the groove?"

"Yep."

"They're headed for high ground. Their boroughs are flooded."

"Are we getting close, Babe? I'm hungry."

Babe pointed up, over his shoulder.

"You should be able to see it from here. It looks like the inside of a big bell."

"Yeah, I see it. What's it called again?"

"The Soul Catcher."

"What's a Soul Catcher?"

"You'll see when we get there."

Hunter watched Babe step onto the flat stone under the Soul Catcher. It didn't look like the rest of the mountain, which was sandstone (he'd been told). This looked more like rusty metal.

Babe knelt down and crawled under the bell. Hunter followed, and they both stood in the darkness. The boy's heart pounded. He found the old man's hand and held it tight.

"Don't be afraid," Babe told him. "Be very quiet."

Hunter didn't notice the ringing in his ears at first. But it got steadily louder.

"Babe?"

He felt Babe give his hand a reassuring squeeze.

"Shhh."

The ringing changed gradually into a sound, like static.

"ssssss…Hunter?…ssssss."

It wasn't Babe's voice. Hunter forgot to hold his bladder. Warm urine ran down his leg.

"Who's that, Babe?"

"ssssss…is that…Hunter?"

"Yes Eric."

It was Babe's voice.

"This is your son, Hunter."

But Hunter heard it in his head. Not through his ears.

"Hunter - meet your father, Eric."
Hunter yelled out:
"What the…"
He tried to run, but Babe held him inside the Soul Catcher.
"sssss We hear you boy sssss you don't have to yell."
"Grandpa, John?"
"sssss Yep sssss. You don't even have to talk."

Hunter caught on and tuned out the static.
"So you can read my mind?'
Several voices answered in unison.
"Yes."
"Hunter Strongbow - you look just like your dad did at that age."
"It's Hunter Strong, Grandpa."
To which Eric asked:
"How come nobody told me she changed his name."
Babe answered first.
"I didn't know. How come you didn't tell him, John?"
John answered Babe.
"I didn't know either, Dad."

The reality of the situation set in for Hunter.
"Wait a minute. I thought you two were dead?"
His father tried to explain.
"We're only dead out there son. As near as I can figure from my Navy training, this place is some kind of cavity resonator."
"Cava-who?"

Grandpa John took over.
"You're confusing the boy. It's simple, Hunter. Brains smoke. Soul Catcher catches smoke from brains."

Hunter nodded.
"Pretty simple, alright."

113

"Now be quiet John," Babe told his dead son. "Let the boy talk to his father."

"Dad?"

"I'm here, Hunter."

"How many people…I mean souls, are in here?"

"All the Strongbow men are in here. But you can't hear most of them, because we sorta use ourselves up, talking to the living. The more you come here when you're alive, the longer you stay around. Babe's gonna be in here forever."

They all laughed.

"How many times did you come here, Dad?"

"Only twice."

"In that case, we better get to the point."

"I told you he was smart," Babe interrupted.

"Dad; why'd you leave us?"

"Because I loved you both so much that I wanted you to have a safe country to grow up in. So I joined the Navy."

"Okay - I guess. What happened to you?"

"Babe saw this on the news and showed it to me."

Eric showed Hunter part of his helicopter crash.

"God took me home to be with Him."

"Why would God do that?"

"I guess I was too messed up to stay here on earth?"

"But why would He let you crash in the first place?"

"In the beginning, our Creator made everything perfect. But He gave us free will, so that we could choose to love Him; rather than making us like robots, that had to. Some men choose to do evil, rather than love God."

"Who made this place?"

"I think God made it; to keep our peoples' spirits alive."

"What people?"

"The Anasazi."

"Ana…sazi?"

"That's right, son. And Babe is the last full blooded Anasazi."

"Really? What happened to the rest of them?"

Hunter felt sadness well up in four hearts, when his father answered,
"You *are* the rest of them."

Grandpa John lightened the conversation.
"Do you still like baseball?"
Babe answered:
"Of course he likes baseball. You ought'a see him pitch."
"It was just a wolf, Babe."
"That doesn't matter," Eric said proudly. "Let's see what you got."

Hunter was confused.
"Huh?"
"Let me see your windup. Just imagine you're throwing a real ball."
Hunter went through the motion, mentally.
"Not bad. Now think about how you hold the ball for a curve."
Hunter did as he was told..
"Who taught you that?"
"Grandpa."
"I should've known. Your grandpa couldn't pitch his way out of a paper bag. If you let me use your arm, I'll show you how to throw a curve that breaks all over the place."
"Okay, but how…"

Hunter's left arm twitched.
"Whoa - how are you doing that?"
"Relax kid."
"But I'm a righty."
Eric laughed and borrowed his son's body.

"Today you're a lefty. Now pay attention."

Eric threw two pitches. One broke left, and the other broke right.

"That's enough, son," John cautioned. "You're gonna use yourself up."

Hunter felt Babe's hand on his shoulder.

"We're gonna have to leave now."

But Eric asked, with a voice full of excitement:

"How about one quick game before you go. I'll catch for Hunter. Dad; you can bat."

"I'll take the field then," Babe offered.

Hunter took on a right-handed pitcher's stance. Eric crouched behind the plate and signaled a fast ball. John saw it too, of course, and smacked a high line drive over second base. Babe leapt, as he did in his twenties, and snagged it right in the web of his worn leather glove, with a perfect *pop*.

"That one was for you, dad, John laughed. "I won't look at no more signals."

Eric signaled a curve, and since Hunter was only taught a left-handed pitcher's curve, he switched stances and gloves - in his mind.

"No batter, no batter, no batter."

Eric signaled a right breaking curve. Hunter put so much spin on the ball that it broke in front of the plate and arced behind the batter. John was confused and swung anyway.

"Steerike," Eric called out. "But next time make it break over the plate."

Eric signaled a left breaking curve. Hunter squeezed it inside before it broke. John jumped back and spat on the ground.

"You trying to bean me, boy?"

"Ball one," Eric yelled. "Over the plate, son - over the plate."

Hunter wound up and spun off a down breaking, inside curve. John didn't swing. Eric caught the ball right in the pocket, with a loud snap.

"Wow, son..." Eric marveled. "...you catch on quick. No batter, no batter, no batter."

Hunter wound up - kicked high, and flipped his wrist for a perfect outside curve that broke right over the plate. John swung and missed - cursing as he threw down the bat.

"You're outta here batter," Babe yelled and threw his glove in the air.

The game was over. Four hearts saddened again. Eric hugged his son, for the first time since he was two, and whispered:

"Tell your mom I hid her locket inside my college baseball trophy. And that I love her. I love you, too."

Babe ducked and pulled Hunter toward the edge of the Soul Catcher dome.

"Hey wait a minute," John called. "Let me see that wolf again - up close."

Hunter showed it to him.

"That's not a wolf," John proclaimed. "It's a wolfayote; half timber wolf and half coyote. Big mean sons of bitches. This one's a female, and she's whelping."

"What's whelping?" Hunter asked.

"It means she's breastfeeding her new pups. But she's so skinny, I doubt she has any milk. Bring her closer."

Hunter concentrated.

"See those porcupine quills in her shoulder. She's wounded. She can't hunt. If you don't feed her, she'll die - and soon. She'll die, and so will her pups."

"We didn't bring any wolfayote food Grandpa," Hunter said, sarcastically.

"There are rabbits all over the place."

Hunter remembered the bunnies in the rocks.

"We didn't bring a gun either."

Eric was stern, when he told his son:
"You're a pitcher, aren't you?"

Babe tugged on the boy's hand.
"We have to go now. Save some of them for next time."
"Goodbye, Dad," Hunter said with tears in his eyes. "Goodbye Grandpa."

The dead men waved until Hunter ducked out of the Soul Catcher. And poof - they were gone. Hunter hadn't even realized it was still raining.

Babe and Hunter stood above the groove, where a train of rabbits hopped toward high ground.

"What are you waiting for? Throw the dang rock."

"But babe, they're just innocent bunnies."

"Boy we had rabbit stew for dinner last night. Where did you think it came from?"

"Okay," Hunter moaned, and threw.

"Did you get one?"

"How could I miss?" The boy answered sarcastically.

"Well get a couple more and let's go."

"How do we even know she'll be down there?"

"Because she's starving, that's how I know."

Babe listened while Hunter grudgingly picked off two more.

"That's enough. Now go get em."

Hunter obeyed.

When they reached the fallen staff, sure enough the beastie was waiting.

"Babe, she's waiting for us."

"I hear her. Toss her a rabbit."

Hunter through it and watched the wolfayote rip into it and pull meat from fur. And then, the strangest thing happened. The beast lifted its front paw.

"I think she's begging."

"Well, throw her another rabbit."

The animal made quick work of the second rabbit, and begged again.

"She's still hungry."

"Throw the last one as far as you can."

Hunter threw it and watched. Then he told Babe:

"She took it and ran off"

The lad led on the way down. He picked up the staff and handed it to his great grandpa. A strong gust of wind blew his hair straight back.

"The storm is picking back up," Babe told him. "We'll wait here under a ledge, until it blows over."

But it didn't blow over. An hour passed with rain coming down in buckets. The saturated ground could hold no more water. Rushing streams formed gullies.

"There's too much water, Babe…" the boy yelled over the storm. "… and nowhere to cross."

"I know what it looks like," Babe answered. "And you're right - we'll be washed away, if we try to cross."

Sheets of water ran off the cliffs.

"There's too much water to climb back up."

With water rising above their ankles, Babe yelled out:

"We'll go the way of the wolf."

Hunter took Babe by the arm, and led him in the direction the wolfayote had run. The water was over his knees when they heard her howl.

"Follow the wolf, boy."

They came upon the wolfayote howling on an outcropping. Two pups took shelter under her. But something was wrong.

"Oh no!"

"What's wrong?"

"Some of her pups are drowned. She can't get to them."

"Are any off them still alive?"

"Yeah. One of them is still swimming."

"Can you reach it?"

"If I hold onto your stick, I can."

"Well take the other end and get to it."

Hunter held onto the end of the staff and jumped in.

"It's over my head."

"Okay - hold on."

Babe groaned as he held Hunter's head above water.

"Hurry, boy - you're heavy."

"Wait I can't reach…"

Hunter went under. Then he felt Babe lift him back up.

"Do you have it? Answer me, boy."

Hunter coughed up water before answering:

"Got em."

Babe pulled him up onto the outcropping, where he took the pup, up to its mother. All three pups followed their mother away from the pool.

"I think I see a way to the road, Babe."

"Are you sure we can make it?"

"No."

"Then follow the wolf."

The rain quieted to a drizzle as they approached the top of the small mesa.

"We're close," the boy whispered. "Put down your stick, so we don't scare her."

Hunter inched closer to the wolfayote family.

"I see the porcupine quills."

"I forgot my knife," Babe whispered. "Boy? Where are you?"

"Shhh," Hunter whispered back.

Hunter reached a hand into the animal's space. A rumble came from deep in her chest. But Hunter didn't stop. The rain soaked wolfayote turned teeth to the boy…and licked his hand.

Hunter stroked her narrow snout, and followed her wide scruffy neck, down to her wounded shoulder. He touched a quill, and it moved freely in a badly infected pus pocket. He pulled it free, and the oozing infection wafted sickeningly up his nostrils.

The wolf wined and hunter threw up. Babe whispered:
   "You alright over there?"
   "We're fine," Hunter whispered back.

The other five quills came out just as easily. The she-wolf licked him on the cheek. Hunter rose and moved slowly back to his elder.
   "I got the quills out, but I think it's infected."
   "I know," Babe answered. "I can smell it. Look around for a cactus, with big flat leaves."
   "I see one."
   "Can you get to it?"
   "Easy."
   "Take my stick and break off a piece."

Hunter slid down the outcropping into waste high water with a splash.
   "Uh oh."
   "What?"
   "It's deeper than I thought."
   "Come back."
   "No. I can do it."

He waded his way to the cactus and…
   "Oh, shit a snake!"
   "Just let him pass, boy. He ain't lookin for food - just dry land."

Hunter waited until the snake swam far, and then beat the cactus, with the staff, until a piece hung off. He twisted it free and sloshed back to high ground.

"Here you go, Babe. Sorry I cussed."

"Nevermind that. Hold out your hand."

Babe scraped out green pulp with his finger nails and rubbed it on Hunter's palm.

"Smear this on the infection, if she'll let you."

Hunter marched boldly back to the wolfayote, just now realizing that she was almost as tall as him. She lay down as he approached and wagged her bushy tail. Hunter stroked the cactus salve onto her wounds, as the puppies started to nurse.

The sun angled low in the west.

"It's getting dark, Babe. What are we gonna do?"

"Can you swim?"

"Grandpa, John, taught me when I was six."

"Can you still see the tree?"

"Yes, but the road is closer"

"The rain's let up. Say goodbye to your friend and let's get, while the gettin is good."

Hunter pet the creature on the back, like a pet, and said goodbye. He slid into the water and reached up a hand.

"Let's go, Babe."

Hunter led great-grandfather through the waste high water and onto a mud bank, where they both slipped and fell down. Hunter helped Babe up, and carefully stepped through the ankle deep mud.

"Dang it!"

"What now boy?"

"I lost my shoe."

"We'll get you a new one tomorrow. Keep going."

The mud gave way to high ground where they walked to within rock throwing distance of the road. Hunter didn't even have to tell Babe, when they came to the last rushing stream.

"How wide is it?"

"Too wide." the boy answered. "We won't make it."

"Find the narrowest place. And I'll help you across with my stick."

Hunter led the way to the narrows.

"I'm scared, Babe," he shouted over the rushing water. "The water is moving really fast."

"Is it wider than my stick is long?"

"Twice as wide."

"We don't wanna be out here in the dark, if it rains again. I'll hold onto something and stretch you as far as I can."

Babe tapped around for something to cling to.

"This'll do it."

And he grabbed it, a cactus, purposefully and stepped into the swift current.

"That's gotta hurt," Hunter joked as he took the end of the staff and backed into the rushing water.

He was halfway across and the water wasn't nearly even up to his waist.

"You're gonna make it," the old man called out. "You hear me, boy?"

"Hey, I'm almost to the other side. I'm gonna swim for it."

"No. Wait!"

Too late.

"Ahhh!" Hunter screamed as the water swept him off his feet.

He saw Babe jump in after him as he washed away. Though he was beaten by rocks, and gurgling for air, his worry was for old man Babe.

"Baaabe! Baaabe!"

Mercifully, Hunter was pushed past the rocks and on to a smooth surface, where he righted himself in a dog paddle. He saw the road, off to his right.

"God, please help Babe," he prayed.

Up, down, up - over slippery stone, Hunter rode the rapids. Then down and down again. His stomach was in his throat. Cold water took his strength. But there, in the distance, he saw a tree fallen along the shoreline. He grabbed it, but something in his right shoulder tore. Strength all but gone, he resolved to meet his Maker…when his shirt caught on a branch.

"Help!" He called out toward the road. "Heeellllp!"

The water tried to take him back, when a voice within said:

"Today you're a lefty."

He grabbed the branch, with renewed strength in his left arm, and pulled himself out of the current and waited for Babe. The old man washed by, face down, far out of Hunter's reach.

Rallying all that was left in him, Hunter staggered to his feet, and ran along the road next to the rushing water. He ran until he couldn't run anymore. He fell to his knees and cried. He'd failed the man who taught him courage. He wasn't a Brave, after all.

But he stood up anyway, and walked. He'd find Babe's body and take him home. And right there, around the first bend, Hunter saw the wolfayote jerking at something in the water.

The animal dragged Babe's limp body onto shore by his shirt.
"Baaaabe!"
The boy fell on his great grandfather's chest. The wolfayote howled. Babe coughed and spit up water and blood.

Hunter dragged him to the road, where he recovered well enough to walk. The wolfayote followed for a spell. Hunter looked back with a grateful heart, and she was gone.

The Soul Catcher: The End

Maybe I Died

Michael Kent

Maybe I died that day. How else could I explain what's become of my life in such a short time. I could tell you who I was, and give you the exact details of my life. But married or not, kids or not, black, white, male or female; you better be prayed up. This could happen to you.

As I write this, I'm deciding whether or not to tell you the true story. It's more bizarre than anything I could make up anyway. Maybe you won't even know the difference.

Six weeks ago my life was as good as a *saved* person with sinful baggage could get. I had the career I dreamed about as a kid. When I came home, I was glad to be pulling up in the driveway. So I was driving a putt-putt, but it was foreign, it wasn't that old, and it was acceptable at any stoplight if it was clean. And I was expecting enough money in the next week to put almost half down, on a brand-new Lexus.

I'm not superficial - just trying to paint a picture. I love my spouse. I'm proud of my kids. We're still just about even with the pool man and the gardener. The Bible tells me to pay the laborers before the sun goes down.

We'd made it through Christmas. For the first time in my recollection, I did Christmas shopping without a credit card. Now just so we're on the same page; doing Christmas, is just about the most ridiculous way I can think of to celebrate the Savior's birth. But I lied to my kids about Santa Clause just like you did.

Ok, so back to what you want to know. What happened was…wait this is funny and I didn't mean for it to be. Anytime you hear an explanation that begins with *what happened was*, it's usually BS - right? So I'll tell you this part just like it happened.

I'm a bodybuilder. I'm in pretty good shape, I guess. But you probably wouldn't be able to tell that I've been doing it, like forever. I have…had a really hectic schedule. Me and my baby, both commuted on the 'tore up', too many cars, not enough lanes, Los Angeles freeway system, for five hours every day. The point being, that I don't have time to go to the gym.

Anyway, I was working out that day; just about six weeks ago. I had mixed up the routines, trying to add some oomph to my stuff. I have this contraption I work out in. I ended up with it when I moved from the townhouse to the apartment on the beach.

Hold on right here, just for a minute. The apartment on the beach. That was the coolest, sweetest, tightest in a low key way, place I ever lived. You could see the Pacific Ocean out of every window. In the morning you might see a porpoise seemingly jumping up out of the living room floor. I met my sweetheart online, when I lived there. I remember saying in my profile that I could see the ocean out of every window. It was a Christian website. Somebody wrote back:

"Get closer to Jesus, and it won't matter what you can see out of your window."

What a dork. I am close to Jesus. But she was right.

So this thing - this bodybuilding station was put together from pieces, to fit on the balcony of the oceanfront apartment. Now it's in my attached garage. It's a cage, about the size of a large refrigerator. The cage has a pull-up bar across the top. The sides, back, and front are empty; with just the pillars in the corners for support. The pillars have holes from top to bottom, so you can position the pegs that hold the Olympic barbell. There's a picture of it, in the intro.

Here's the key point. The cage has rods that you can slide through the holes, from front to back, and they act as a spotter. For those of you who are not gym rats, or cats, or vixens; the spotter is the person who picks the weight up off your dumb behind when you've put on so much that you can't pick it up off yourself. Picture this:

"Hey buddy...arrgh...a little help here!" Said the sweaty lady on the bench with the bar stuck across her upper abdomen.

For those of you who do go to the gym, you know that your muscles grow by pushing them past their comfort zone. So anyway, there's a portable bench that I put in the rack when I do upper body. I've done it a thousand times. I put the spotter rods just lower than my ribcage. I rep out and roll the bar, along my ribcage, toward my neck. The bar rolls onto the rods, and I slide out from under it, and rest way too long before the next set.

That day I was mixing it up though. I took the rods out so I could lift the bar from the floor. Those are called deadlifts. Something told me I shouldn't be working out on the Sabbath. Gee, I wonder who that was? We're not under the law. But I should've listened.

I remember (and this is also key), it was the first Sunday, after the first Sunday in my life when I had enough faith to actually tithe. I had decided that ten percent of every dollar that passed through my bank account was going into the basket.

I pulled those rods out all the time to do floor exercises. This time something said:

"Move em out of the way, so you don't trip over them."

You guessed it - out of sight, out of mind. I forgot to put the rods back in. I slid the bench in the cage, just like always. Put too much weight on the bar, laid down and picked the loaded bar up off the pegs. Now, down - one, two, and back on the pegs. Now for three reps. One, two, two and a half... not gonna work... put it down on the rods. Remember - I'd done it at least a thousand times.

Funny thing - my Pastor says that sometimes, before the alter call.

"We're all just one breath or one accident away from the here-after. You might get onto the freeway and never get off. You might do something you've done a thousand times before. But this time something goes wrong. You might not get another chance to answer His call. Don't leave here today, not knowing where you'll spend eternity."

I still didn't realize I'd forgotten to put the rods back in. I rolled the bar toward my neck - just like always. The heavy Olympic bar pressed into my throat. The entire weight was on my neck before I realized what was going on. I can still feel it.

It's what I felt in the nightmare I just woke up from - the one where I felt like I was slipping away into insanity. I'm saved. It was a bad dream - right? I can't go back to sleep. I probably will when night rolls back around. But you won't know one way or the other - will you?

The weight rolled fully onto my neck, pushed my head down behind the end of the bench, and was about to lock into the groove between the back of my jawbone and my ears. In essence, I had hung myself. The bar was already jammed against the back pillars of the cage. It had nowhere to go but down. And it was way too heavy for me to pick it back up. I couldn't even lift it again when it was on my chest.

What should have happened was that I'd hold out as long as I could, until the bar snapped my neck and stretched it to the floor. My family was supposed to find me mangled in a death trap. That's what the *enemy* had planned.

What actually happened (and I believe this with all my heart) was that angels lifted the bar off my throat and pulled the whole bench, with me on it, out from under it. The bar fell to the floor so loudly that Jackie, who was inside the house, wondered if I was alright.

I went over it in my mind. What had just happened? Was it possible that I had picked it up off my own throat? I remembered pushing up on it and turning my head to the side before it locked into that groove. But it felt like it was no heavier than a toddler. It was like I had a spotter.

What if I died that day? What if this parody of my former life is just the poorly remembered pieces of a dream, being dreamt, as I drift away at the other end of my silver cord? In that case none of this is real. I'm not writing this story. And you'll never read it. Good thing I'm prayed up.

Things began to change almost immediately. I tried to explain what had happened in the accident; to my family, to friends. I guess you just had to be there. But you weren't. The first change I noticed is that my faith in God had gone way up. I mean like off the Richter scale. I no longer cared about the things that used to worry me; who could, after being saved by angels.

We've had a saying in my family for years now. It comes from Psalms ninety-one. I encourage you to go to the Bible, yourself, and look it up; like the Bereans, in Acts, who searched the scriptures daily to see if the things they heard were true.

So my family says:

"Angels all around you," when we leave each other's company.

Psalms ninety-one says that God will give His angels charge over you; to hold you up, so you don't even stub your toe.

A few days later I went into town. That's what I call driving into LA. I was going to check on the deal that was going to net an honest fourteen thousand dollars. When I got there my friend had bad news.

"We've been doing business for a long time now - right?" He asked rhetorically. "And I've always got your back. You know that. But this time the numbers didn't go your way. I'm sorry."

I wasn't even mad. I told him about the angels saving my life. He actually understood. We talked about a new strategy that would swing things in my direction. I can't believe what came out of my mouth.

"What's the point in tithing if I still bend the rules?"

That would be like I didn't trust God to handle His Malachi three-ten business. I gotta tell you, I didn't expect doing the right thing to feel so good. Tithing made me a more honest person. A couple of days after that, I was still smarting from being so honest. I was at this kids' sporting event, and the ticket taker gave me back too much change. I could've used it too, but I gave it back. That felt good too.

My Bible study is teaching the life of Moses this year. The big lesson for the Israelites was that they had to obey God, in order for Him to be in their presence at the center of their camp. Me and my love both go to that Bible study, and we jumped into the concept of God at the center of our lives, with both feet. Just so you know; the first question I ever asked my love wasn't about signs or hobbies, or favorite places.

"How's your walk with Christ?" was my icebreaker.

Tell you what single people. You try *that*, and people who ain't right will stutter and move right on out of your path. That goes for male or female. God was, and still is, at the center of our camp.

Now about that job. It had been my strength and my identity for a good long time. It was the source of my stability. I might have admitted that I wasn't the mover and shaker I once was. But I didn't need to be. The truth is that I never was. God had always been my Provider.

As I look back over my life, anything that had been my idea never ended up like I thought it should. My chooser has been broken for a long time. The good and lasting things in my life just sort of overtook me, like the blessings from God to the righteous. And don't get it twisted - my righteousness comes from my acceptance of Christ as my Lord and Savior.

Romans says that God had chosen me, from before the foundations of the earth. Maybe He blessed me in advance because He knew that I would accept His Son. So, needless to say, I hadn't chosen this career. I had something more glamorous in mind. But I had come to depend on that job as my provider.

Never show up at a four-thirty meeting on Friday afternoon - especially in a recession. And doubly especially, when there's been a merger. They said what they had to say:

"Your function will no longer be needed after the end of the month."

And then they said something about a party.

I felt physically ill. I had been for a long time, but I was motivated to work through it because I had a passion for the cause. I can't say I didn't understand. They had to trim the fat. But knowing that they saw me as fat - well that's a whole nother emotion. Alright - strike two. But we still have a check coming in, so we'll be ok.

It might be hard for some to understand how we kept tithing after that. After all, God said He would rebuke the devourer, and pour us out so many blessings that we wouldn't have room to receive it. The two of us touch, and pray over the envelope, before we drop it in the basket.

I remember reading about the man of God, who asked the widow to make him a cake, with her last portion of grain. She and her son were going to eat it, and then starve to death. But she trusted God, and fed the man. The man anointed her remaining cup of oil, and it multiplied so abundantly that she and her son sold it and lived off the profits throughout the entire famine.

Our tithes are seeds planted in God's kingdom. They provide, in the same way as the widow's oil provided for her neighbors. They will bless others before they bless us. But we have faith that we will be blessed, because we stand on God's word.

And He cannot lie. In this time of worldwide recession, teetering on the brink of depression, we have chosen to live in God's economic system, not that of the world's.

"How?" My darling asked. "How will we make it through?

I answered, "We're gonna *give* our way through."

I had been off work for a week. Between doctor visits, I rested and enjoyed the home that He has given us. The members of our household came and went. Sometimes I helped with the dropping off and picking up. Other times I just loaned out my putt-putt. I hadn't intended to write a book. It just happened.

The first book I wrote got jacked. It got turned into a made for TV movie. Man, I still remember how bad I felt when people told me they saw my story on TV. I suffer through a sequel every year. I had taken out a copyright, but I didn't get the copyright insurance. Two lawyers told me the same thing.

"You stand to get fifty thousand dollars if you sue."
"Ok, so how much will it cost to sue?"
"Fifty thousand dollars."
This time I'll get the insurance.

I had an idea what I wanted it to be about. By the way, this is not that book. I finished that one yesterday. And that's part of the misty dream that has become my life. Who writes a novel in six weeks - I mean what regular person? My first book took two years to write. I knew what I wanted it to be about - sort of. And then there's this thing I do. I always know the ending, before I start.

The first time I wrote the ending in detail. Oops. That's part of the reason it took two years. I had written myself into a tight corner, so it took a lot of time to reconcile the plot, to the ending. This time (the second book), I just loosely captured some of the dialog lines and narrative. I know the ending of the story you're reading now, but I haven't written it down at all.

For me, the hard part is writing the beginning. Forgive my stream of thought here, but I need to tell you that I wasn't saved when I (we) wrote my first book. The book was pretty edgy. I had a coauthor - which is the other reason it took two years. She wrote the beginning of that book.

The book I just finished didn't start anything like I would've thought up. It started with a name that came to me in a dream. I woke up saying it - saying her name. And as I went through my unemployed day, she told me who she was. By noon, she was telling me her story. All I did was type it out. It gives me the creeps just thinking about what I just wrote (right now). During the course of the day, she told me the rest of her story.

Ok wait. I'm not hearing voices. I don't mean it like that. What I mean is that every story I write, tells itself to me. I just go through my day, and the story tells itself. I was done with hers by four o'clock that afternoon. It was chapter one. I read it out loud, when I was done. I read her words, in her voice. She told a tale of demons, and gold, and the souls of the newly dead. It was downright chilling. I wrote it, and it still creeped me out.

I'll be darned if *that* wasn't the night that the haunting started. We have a relatively large house. Lots of people come and go. Some nights many of the rooms remain dark. That night, I was working on chapter two. We had been worried about finances and family wellbeing. Most of us, to some extent, were afraid of the dark. In spite of that, my sweetie wants to turn off all the lights to keep down the electric bill.

Little Morgan was sneaking out of the kitchen, to take food upstairs. Mama had told all of them, in no uncertain terms, that they were not to eat in the bedrooms. Little Morgan was the defiant one; always in trouble, and always had an excuse. There was no excuse that night. Morgan screamed (so loud that I almost knocked over the keyboard) and came tearing around the corner, skidded on the tiles and plowed right into me.

"What's wrong Morgan?"

Morgan was looking back as if being chased. I was startled, but not afraid. Pretty often, I don't know who's here and who's not.

"Somebody called me."

"Huh? Somebody called you?"

"They called my name?"

"Who?"

"I don't know!"

"There's somebody outside playing a trick." I said.

Morgan indulged me, as I led the way and we looked out all the downstairs windows.

"I'm trying to tell you - it didn't come from outside."

I swallowed hard.

"That can't be true."

"It was right behind me. It whispered in my ear."

Nobody was here, except for three. The third was an adult, upstairs, fast asleep.

As I worked on chapter two that night, I was keenly aware that I was forcing myself not to look over my shoulder. The truth is that I was a little bit more afraid of the dark after that.

The very next night, there were three of us at home. Morgan was not one of them. Me and my love were upstairs, worried and doubtful. One of us worried about Jackie, the other was doubtful about their career. Jackie was in our office, on the computer. Amari's ears perked toward the door.

"Did you hear Jackie just call me?"

"No. I was just down there. Jackie's got the music turned up on the computer. You wouldn't be able to hear over it."

Amari didn't take my word for it, and went out to the upstairs banister.

"Jackie! Jackie!"

"What?"

"Did you just call me?"

"No!"

When Amari came back in the bedroom, I couldn't help but rub it in.

"Told you."

But that was the second time, in as many days, that a family member heard someone call their name.

Later on that night, I heard Morgan standing outside our bedroom door and calling out to me. I even answered. What a mistake. Morgan wasn't even home that night. The next morning the three of us that were home compared notes. Seems Jackie had an encounter too.

"Somebody called my name too. But I wasn't scared. I went looking for it."

"It?"

"Yeah, it was right behind me. But I saw an angel when I was little, so I wasn't afraid."

Here's where I have to tell you that we had spent many a night blessing our house, and asking God to keep it free of evil. But now they had called four of us, by name, in the last two days. So I went straight into Ephesians six, ten through eighteen mode, and put on the full armor of God. I was preparing to take on the demon government. Guess you'll have to read Ephesians if you don't know what I'm talking about. That's chapter six, verses ten through eighteen.

Next time I went to Bible study, I was going to ask my group for *prayer cover*. In the same way that ground troops in a war would ask for *air cover*. In the same way a woman caught in the rain would need *hair cover*. My group leader questioned me first.

"Have you guys been really worried about anything?"

"Um - yeah! I told you last week that the rug got pulled from under me at work."

It wasn't really as sarcastic as that sounded. My group leader didn't take it that way either.

"You know Tyler - when we worry, we invite the spirit of Worry into our home. And then it watches as we show a lack of faith in God's word."

"If that's the case, we've also invited Fear, Doubt, and Defiance. Any advice?"

"You have to take charge, and you have to get loud. Just like you would if you were throwing anyone else out of your house. You already have that authority. It was given to you by Christ."

That's when I connected the dots. They had called us by name. We were trying to get rid of them by saying:

"Everybody out!"

"Turn on all the lights too," he told me. "Demons love to hang out in dark places, because they know people are afraid of the dark. More fear equals less faith."

I'll use an analogy here. Say you gave a party. You invited your family and closest friends. Suppose that fifty people that you didn't know showed up also. Now, the party is starting to get out of hand. Your neighbors are gonna call the cops at any minute. You've had it - right? You turn off the music and flip on the lights. You get loud.

"That's it! Everybody out!"

You're standing at the door tapping your feet, wondering why some of the people are still making themselves at home. Guess who's still there? I'll wait. Pretend you hear that music from the TV show where you have to guess the question that goes with the answer. The people you invited are still there.

Your, "everybody out" didn't apply to the people you invited.

You have to call them by name.

"That means you too, Troy. Sally - out. Jenifer, why are you still sitting there?"

Get it? They called us by name. We had to disinvite them...by name.

Little Morgan and I rode home from Bible study together that night. It was Morgan who put the final piece in the puzzle in place.

"Morgan - when we get home we have to cast them out by name. They called *us* by name, so we have to call *them* by name. We'll call out Fear, Worry, Doubt, and Defiance. And we'll kick em out."

Morgan paused to process what I'd said. But only for a moment.

"I was *being* defiant, when Defiance whispered in my ear. I was sneaking up to my bedroom with a soda and two bags of chips. You told us not to eat in the bedroom. You tell us that all the time."

The spiritual lights were on now. I was doubtful, when Doubt called my name. Amari was worrying, when worry called. Who knows what Jackie was doing on the computer when the demon called out. When we got home that night:

"Hi Tyler."

"Hey Amari. We figured out why we're being attacked."

"Oh?"

I told Amari the analogy about the party.

"You wanna walk with me while I cast them out, by name?"

"I already blessed the house tonight," Amari replied. "You go ahead."

"You wanna come with me, Morgan?"

"Nope."

So I set out alone. I turned on every light in the house. I got loud. I went through every room, every closet, and cupboard.

"You're not welcome here, Fear. Get out in the name of Jesus. On your way, Worry - this is our house, and we worship Jesus here. Defiance, you go straight to hell. Get out of my house and never come back. The Lord did not give us the spirit of fear, but of power, and of love, and of a sound mind."

On I went through every room. Now this is a Christian household. Five of us were home, and not one person looked at me like I was crazy. My sister-in-law even added to the battle from her own Christian arsenal.

"My Pastor said you have to open the door when you put them out."

I get a kick every time we open the door to give our house a spiritual cleansing. The non-Christian neighbors must think we're bonkers. And probably some of the Christians too.

I'd purposely saved the garage for last. It was the creepiest door to open. I turned on the lights and walked in. I was casting the demons out by name. I got as far as Fear. I started reading the ninety first Psalm.

Our garage is an artwork of organized clutter, constantly being rearranged because of people coming and going. And, also because Amari restores used furniture. When will I ever learn to keep my mouth shut about it?

"What are you gonna do with that piece of dusty old junk?"

"Tyler, when are you gonna learn to trust me?"

Once, Amari bought a glass table with pillars for a base. Amari had a plan but I didn't get it. After every coat of paint that went onto those pillars, I had something to say.

"It looks fine like that. Why are you painting over it?"

Well, I should have shut up. Now we have a beautiful dining table with ivory and cracked gold pillars. Amari bought it for around a hundred dollars. Once the six chairs were reupholstered, I'm sure it would retail for fifteen hundred.

Meanwhile back in the garage. Don't you hate it when an author says that? Ok, I won't do it again. I was pacing and casting out Fear, while reading Psalm ninety-one. I made it about half way, when something in the corner made a racket like an animal that had gotten trapped in the garage. I jumped clear off the floor with both feet. Kobe didn't have nothin on me that night. Something had fallen over with a clatter and a bang.

When my feet returned to earth, I put the Bible down and started cursing the thing in the name of Jesus. I'm telling you, I expected a dog to come out with its tail tucked between its legs. It didn't happen. Not a cat, not even a mouse. I opened the door, and kicked it out, like Amari's sister told me.

I looked in that corner the next day. Nothing was out of place. The empty picnic cooler would have explained the noise, but there it sat, right where we'd put it the week before, when we last rearranged the garage. The same pile of stuff was still stacked on top of it. The fishing tackle boxes were clear on the other side of the garage. There was absolutely nothing there to explain that noise I heard.

I believe Christians have the power to cast out demons. I've done it before. I must tell you that I got saved reading Christian fiction. When the heroine, in Frank Piretti's *Piercing the Darkness*, finally came to understand the need for salvation, I found myself kneeling beside her at the foot of the cross.

I started out being grateful that He died in my place. It was a month before I realized I got to go to heaven. But I knew right off the bat, that I had the authority over dark influences, because of His work on the cross. That's what Christian fiction is usually about. So I knew that *by faith*, I could cast out demons. I just didn't expect them to make such a racket on the way out.

The new book had taken off. It was writing itself, at the rate of five pages a day. I was halfway done in three weeks. The plot was solid, and the groundwork was laid. The characters had taken on lives of their own.

Christian fiction has, built in, bad guys. The bad guys were growing personalities as well. I even had the gall to call out Satan, himself. Maybe I pissed him off. Good thing He, who is in me, is greater than he who is in the world. Jesus stomped out Satan two thousand and some years ago.

A few evenings later, Morgan smelled smoke.
    "Can't you smell that smoke?"
    "No." I said, as I sniffed at the air.
    "Well come over here by the couch. Smell that?"
    "No. I don't smell anything. Stop trippin!"

Later that night, Amari and I were awakened by the smoke alarm in our bedroom. It was doing that dead battery chirp. We didn't bother it though. We just put pillows over our ears. Every thirty seconds it chirped again.

We had fooled with that thing for whole day, a couple of years back. The little green light wasn't working. You know - the one that tells you the battery is good. One of us held the ladder for the other to get up to the vaulted ceiling.

We found the bad wire. Every time we touched that stupid wire, the thing would blare for a minute straight. A chirp every thirty seconds beats the pants off of blaring for a whole minute.

Chirp…chirp…chirp…chirp…chirp.

And it was worse in real life. It went on until fifteen minutes before my love had to get up for work. Then it started back after Amari left; until fifteen minutes before I had to get up.

So now I'm up. Got the ladder out of the garage, and I'm up there fiddling with it. I finally figured out how to disconnect it from the ceiling. No power; it shouldn't be a problem now. I laid it on the bed, where it chirped again. Better have a closer look - right? Ah, so there was a battery. I took it out. I laid the smoke alarm on top of the Bible, on our dresser. Can you believe that sucker still chirped?

Six hours later, after I had gone and come, and gone and come again, it still chirped, intermittently. I can't even say I'm no rocket scientist; because I *was*. None the less, we all pretty much know…IT SHOULDN'T DO THAT! No power, no battery - still chirping. Right there on top of the Bible. No smoke, no power, no battery - still chirping. Ok, whatever.

Next night, in the middle of the night, the smoke alarm outside our room went off. I mean *off* - as in something was burning. It let out a solid wail, for just long enough for my sweetheart to go out and check. Then it stopped. No smoke, different circuit. Not the dead battery chirp, but the something's on fire blare. None of the smoke detectors has ever gone off, since we moved here. But the smoke that Morgan had smelled may have come from a spiritual realm.

Let's do a brief flashback, to a time I'd seen worse; back in the townhouse with my ex. We would hear bumps in the night pretty regularly. I wasn't saved back then. My ex claimed Christ. It was so bad that once we heard knocks on the second story window outside our bedroom. I figured the neighbors had a teenager over. And that the teenager had leaned way over from their second story balcony to ours - way, way over. I jumped up the second time. I was out the balcony door in plenty of time to catch the kid. Nobody there. Imagine that.

Check this out. It got so bad, that we'd hear a tapping on the wall next to our bed. It was actually coming from inside the wall. It could have been rats, I guess. But then it went tapping along the inside of the wall, until it got to the window sill. Then it went to the other side - the other side of the window…the glass window. Then it kept going to the corner, and then around the corner.

There was a computer on the desk in front of that wall. When it got behind the computer, the computer started 'clicking and popping' with electrical noises. It went past the computer, around the next corner, all the way to the bedroom door. Then - you guessed it - it continued tapping on the other side of the door.

Now mind you, me and my ex were looking right at each other. But it wasn't a big deal because it happened almost every night. That night it went all the way around the room and then into the mattress under our feet. You heard me right. I said, *under our feet.*
    "Was that you?"
    "You know, good and well, it wasn't me."
    "Well it wasn't me either."
    No big deal though; we'd seen even worse than that at the townhouse. By the way - we didn't have rats. Long story short; the smoke alarms were not that big a deal.

The doorbell woke me up the next night. Why does everything happen at three AM? We have the traditional super loud, melodious: ding dong, *ding* dong…wait for it …ding dong, *ding* dong.

You didn't actually play that tune in your head, did you? You did, didn't you? Anyway, I heard it at three AM. I knew when I heard it that no one was at the door.

But Ryan was still out. I went to the door, just in case. Nobody was at the door. I had gotten there in plenty of time for whomever it was to still be standing there; or at least waiting by a car with the engine running. You know who it was - right? I didn't open the door. That would have meant I was inviting them back in. Maybe that had been them trying to get back in through the electrical wiring, and they set off the smoke alarm. Naaa.

The attacks got serious after that. That is, if you disregard the near fatal weight lifting accident. Somebody in our family must be on the verge of doing mighty works, in the name of the Lord. When we discussed it - each of us thought it was them.

Amari was driving back from town. Casey was in the passenger's seat. My cell phone rang.

"Baby it's me."

"What's wrong?"

"A truck almost turned over on us."

"Oh my God - a truck?"

"A tanker truck."

"Are you guys ok?"

"Yeah, we're ok. Casey wake up! Did you see that?"

"See what?"

That reminds me of another time Casey didn't see the near catastrophe. Don't lose our place - I'll come back in a minute.

It was a year earlier - but I need to start two years before that. Back when I first bought the putt-putt. The lock on the rear left door would always get stuck.

"Open the door for me," Morgan would ask, from the back seat.

"Open it yourself, Morgan."

"I can't; the lock is stuck."

"What are you - two?"

"I'm not two. Your car is just whack."

"Why don't you just sit on the other side?"

"I like *this* side."

We must have had that same conversation a hundred times. That lock still sticks, but we don't complain anymore. You see, one day we were at a stop light in the hood. I was driving. Morgan and Casey were in the back. I saw a guy crossing the street behind my car, but I thought he was trying to catch the bus that was at the corner, on the other side of the car. It was hot that evening, so the windows were half down.

The guy wasn't trying to catch the bus. He had his head in the back window, trying to open the lock, that closed automatically when the car was in 'drive'. We were being quietly carjacked, and the only one who knew it was Morgan. I was scrolling through the calls on my cell. Casey was staring out the window in the direction of the bus. Morgan, the defiant one, was fighting the guy through the window.

Finally I heard:

"What are you doing up there?"

In other words, why can't you see this guy in the window trying to get in our car? I looked in the rear view.

"Oh snap!"

That's not what I really thought. I saw an opening to my left, and peeled off, with the guy still hanging out the window. I was probably up to twenty miles an hour, when the guy fell off. He flipped end over end, down the street. Funny, he came to rest, sitting up with his legs crossed. And Casey didn't see any of it. As was often the case with Casey.

I'd had a premonition, earlier in the day, that someone needed to jump in my car to get away from a dangerous situation. I didn't remember it in time to help the guy who was trying to get in my car. Besides, he hadn't asked for help. The moral of the story is that the stuck lock saved us. That, and feisty Morgan. I had always complained about both. Now they were both saviors.

Here it comes - Romans eight-twenty-eight:

"All things work together for good, for those who love God; for those who are called to His purpose."

Like I said, we don't complain about the stuck lock anymore.

And now, back to the reason I told the story in the first place,

"Did you see that Casey?"

"See what?"

Once again, Casey missed the whole thing. So my baby was on the phone describing to me how this tanker truck tipped over on the car.

"It tipped over, and we were right under it. God - how would I have explained the accident to Casey's mom?"

"You mean it came up off of its wheels?"

"Yes. It tipped over, and there wasn't anywhere to go. I usually keep a way out when I drive. Next thing I knew, the car was somewhere else, and the truck was back on all of its wheels."

"Babe, remember when I told you the angels had saved me from hanging myself in the workout cage? It was the angels. They held up the truck, and moved your car out of the way."

Amari says I tend toward the dramatic. And that I never met an exaggeration that I didn't like. This time Amari agreed. It must have been angels. How else could you explain it?

Maybe I'm dying in the workout cage. Maybe my neck is stretching to the floor, and all these imaginings are racing through my brain in a split second.

Four of us went to dinner, on the Saturday of that week. Nothing fancy; just a buffet where everybody could have whatever they liked. Casey and Morgan would probably have an eating contest, the way they always did.

Earlier that day, I'd talked with Deshon, who was away at college. Deshon, an 'A' student, is a junior at a prestigious southern college. We traded greetings and well-wishes. Everything was fine.

Morgan and Casey piled their plates high. Amari and I wondered how much more we could take. We were somber but prayerful. I was near the end of my rope.

"I just don't know if I can take one more piece of bad news."

We take turns holding each other up. Two traveling together, Jesus said, is better than one travelling alone. If one falls, the other can help him up. At any given time, one of us has been able to see. Unlike the blind leading the blind, where both will fall in a pit.

At one point during the meal, Morgan looked perplexed.

"Why is the table shaking?"

"The table's not shaking."

"Put your hand right here."

I did. The table was vibrating - but only in that one spot. Let me see if I can think of something to describe the sensation. Ok, got it…an earthquake. I looked up at the lamp that hung above the table. If you've ever been in an earthquake, you know that a hanging lamp or chandelier will keep swinging for a long time. It wasn't swinging.

The next thing you would look for, was the kid sitting in the booth behind you, kicking his seat. I looked. The booths weren't attached. The table wasn't even attached to the floor. It was attached to the wall next to me. Why was it shaking way over there by Morgan? Amari couldn't feel it - or didn't want to.

The next morning was a Sunday. Deshon called again. The phone rung while I was still dreaming, so the conversation started with my dream.

"You woke me up. I was dreaming about the rapture. I saw Him, I really saw Him, in all His glory; coming amidst the clouds. The saints were with Him. He lit up the whole sky. The believers all ran outside jumping for joy, because they knew what was about to happen."

I went on like that, without Deshon interrupting. I didn't expect what I heard in reply.

"I died the other day."

"You died?"

"Yeah, I died. My friend kicked in the door and brought me back."

It wouldn't be the first near-death experience in the family. My mother died four times.

One time she was on the phone with another of my ex's. I told you in the beginning that I had baggage. Mom couldn't stand that ex. They couldn't stand each other. I don't even know why they were on the phone that day. What I do know is that Mom was having a severe asthma attack. My ex hung up the phone and called nine-one-one, in Las Vegas. We lived in Inglewood California. The paramedics got there in time to revive my mom. Her heart had stopped. She had turned blue.

On another occasion my mom had just met a new friend. My mother was a saint. By that I mean she was genuinely friendly. The two women talked for hours. When they parted company that night, the woman invited my mom to breakfast. Mom gave her the address, and the woman showed up the next morning. She knocked on the door. The door was unlatched and it swung open.

"Hello. Is anyone home?"

The woman came inside and found my mother on the kitchen floor. *Dead*, on the kitchen floor. The woman happened to be a nurse, and was able to resuscitate my mother. Mom later told me that the woman was an angel. It wasn't until just this moment that Mom's description of the woman took on real meaning. You see, I haven't told anyone that Mom's savior was an angel, until the angels saved me.

Her room-mate revived her, on yet a different occasion. No one was there the last time she died. But when my sister and I got to her Las Vegas apartment, her insurance papers were open on her desk. She knew it was the end. At her Las Vegas funeral, I eulogized her.

"My mother's spirit outgrew the confines of her fragile body."

I met dozens of her friends before I took her body home to Detroit. Every one of them said she was their good, good friend."

So, when Deshon spoke of dying, it didn't seem out of the ordinary to me. Deshon had been very sick, and didn't have insurance coverage in that state. We traded stories on the phone. I reminded Deshon of the time my mother called us from heaven.

I always figured Mom had died and come back so many times that she remembered the way. She never mentioned any lights at the end of a tunnel, or anything like that. And I never asked. I wasn't saved when she died that final time.

She had come back several times. I think she must have gotten permission from God, because I was in danger. Satan would have had her tell me to blow my brains out. I won't tell you every story. Just the one I have in common with Deshon (and Morgan too, I guess).

She usually came to me in my sleep. She came in one of those dreams that you can tell isn't just a dream. I've had many of those; including the one that foretold her death. Three weeks before she died, I dreamed I was at her funeral.

So she came, in this dream, and told me I could call her on the phone. She said her phone bill was always paid. I knew the number. It was one of the ones we'd had when we lived in Detroit. And she knew that I knew. One mothers' day I woke up with Morgan, who was three at the time, and in my bed. I dialed that number.

Now you know you can't go dialing just any old phone number. It will either be disconnected, or it will be a wrong number. Neither of those was the case. Someone picked up the other end, but they didn't say a word. I waited for a moment, to make sure.

"Happy Mother's Day, Mom." I said crying.

Then I gave the phone to Morgan.

"Tell your grandmother happy Mother's Day."

"Happy Mother's Day, Grandma."

I took the phone back from Morgan. Then the person on the other end hung up.

That's the part involving me and Morgan. Here's the part that involved me and Deshon.

One night Deshon was crying.

"I'm so sad. I can't stop crying. I think it's because I never got to say goodbye to Grandma, all those years ago."

I consoled Deshon, with the story about the spiritual telephone. And that Morgan and I had actually used it to talk to my mother. The very next morning, I was dropping everybody off at school. This is back when I was single. I had just dropped off Tory, and only Deshon and I were left in the car. My cell phone rang. It was my ex; the one who had saved Mom's life by calling the Vegas paramedics.
"Your mother just called me."
My heart lit up, like the sky in my dream of the rapture.

My ex went on.
"I wasn't asleep. But I wasn't quite awake either. A phone rang. I don't know how, but I answered it."

I was in drug induced depression at the time. I was taking an experimental compound of very powerful drugs, to treat a life-threatening illness. And I was on my way to work to tell my managers what I thought of them. What I thought, was that they were conspiring to make me a scapegoat for their failed plans. I was depressed and so was Deshon.
"Your mother was on the phone. She said to tell you that everything is going to work out alright."

I had just told Deshon about the spiritual telephone the night before.
"Tell Deshon, what you just told me."
That phone call brought light into our hearts that day.

Talking about it *again*, on the phone with Deshon that Sunday morning, brought light into our hearts all over again. How was I to know that Deshon was delusional; in the midst of a nervous breakdown? I just added a spiritual dimension to Deshon's already delusional mind. I would see Deshon two days later... in an Alabama asylum.

I must have been on about chapter twenty of my new book, when the phone rang. Things were about to get ugly; in the book, *and* in real life. The devil has used the same bag of tricks since before the Garden of Eden. I'll remind you again. You don't have to take what I say as Gospel. God gave us His written word that He promised to preserve for us. Look it up in the Bible, yourself. Ok, so let's get to Satan's big stick - his total contempt for God.

Satan Thrown Out of Heaven - in Revelation 12:

"And war broke out in heaven: Michael and his angels fought with the dragon; and the dragon and his angels fought, but they did not prevail, nor was a place found for them in heaven any longer. So the great dragon was cast out, that serpent of old, called the Devil and Satan, who deceives the whole world; he was cast to the earth, and his angels were cast out with him."

I don't want to cut and paste scripture, just to add to the page count. That said; some things are foundational. Satan was cast out. He was defeated in heaven. He had no say so; no get back, no do-over. We are God's greatest treasure. Look at these two parables, from Mathew, chapter thirteen.

The Parable of the Hidden Treasure:

"Again, the kingdom of heaven is like treasure hidden in a field, which a man found and hid; and for joy over it, he goes and sells all that he has and buys that field."

The Parable of the Pearl of Great Price:

"Again, the kingdom of heaven is like a merchant seeking beautiful pearls, who, when he had found one pearl of great price, went and sold all that he had and bought it."

I don't mean to get into a scriptural debate. I'm not a clergyman. I'm not even a deacon. I'm just a plain old Christian. If we take the pearl in these parables to be mankind, the finder of the pearl to be God, and the payment of 'all He has' to be Christ. That paints the picture of mankind being of supreme importance to God. We really need look no further than John three-sixteen. What would *you* sacrifice the life of *your* only child for?

God is omnipotent. In and of ourselves, we are finite and feeble. God loves us. Satan hates God. You do the math. By the associative property, Satan hates us like cockroaches on a birthday cake. His enmity toward God, transfers directly to us, and he will stop at nothing to destroy us. That's the big stick. Blind, raging hatred. That's what fuels his attacks.

Look back at your own human life. What or whom have you destroyed, in the heat of rage. Look at our prisons. They're overflowing with humanity that fell while in rage.

Look back at the passage from Revelation, chapter twelve. It called the devil, Satan, who deceives the whole world. That's one of his mainstays - deception. He twists the reality of God's creation and of God's word, just enough so that it remains a viable truth in our minds. The result is paranoia, fear and desperation.

He doesn't use the boogeyman, or toss a Great White shark in your bedroom. He uses the fear of economic insecurity, spurred on by the onslaught of news about recession. He uses the fear of marital infidelity, spurred on by jealous rumors. He deceived Eve, by slightly changing God's word and then tempting her to question it.

There are mountains of books regarding the devil's schemes against humanity. This was not meant to be one of those. These are memoirs from the battlefield. Here, we care about saving as many people as possible.

We are not so much concerned with the head of the demon government, as we are with the sixth level imps and trolls that are attacking us. Satan is not omnipresent. He cannot be everywhere, personally attacking all of us, at the same time. He deploys his legions, according to levels of authority.

That brings me to the point of this tangent. After we've put on the armor, and thwarted all his attacks, there remains one subtle and insidious weapon that waits like a time bomb. When all else fails, he can pit us against each other. When those seeds grow fruit, we are doomed. Jesus Himself said that a house divided against itself could not stand.

I was working on chapter twenty. The demons were about to begin their psychological assault on the heroine. The phone rang. It was a friend of Deshon's, from college.

"Deshon is in the emergency room..." The next words stood out from the rest. "...about to be committed."

The friend's description of Deshon's mental state is difficult to put into words. But it was like the spiritual conversations that Deshon and I had, that Sunday, had been thrown into a psychotic meat grinder. That, along with age regression and some very bizarre behavior.

Financial instability, haunting, outright assault - now this. One of us was being attacked on the inside. How was this possible? We're saved. I saw Deshon baptized in the name of Jesus, with my own eyes. I heard the sinner's prayer come out of Deshon's mouth.

I went off. I still didn't get how bad it was.

"Put Deshon on the phone!"

"Deshon," I said to the 'A' student who was about to be tucked away in a mental health ward. "You can't be down there casting your pearls before swine. They'll trample it under foot and turn and tear you apart."

Silly me - quoting scripture to a psychotic.

I called my Bible study group leader.

"I won't be at Bible study tonight,"

Then I gave an update on the series of attacks.

"Please ask the group to pray for us."

I'm sure it was those prayers that helped us through the coming turbulence.

My eighteen-year-old, Tory, and I packed enough clothes for a few days and headed out on a sleepless rollercoaster of cars, planes, and hospital waiting rooms. We managed to navigate the treacherous straights of emergency air travel, finally ending up at the Alabama mental facility, where Deshon had been placed on three day hold.

I'll only share with you three realities of that part of the ordeal:

One - Deshon had been a college student just twenty-four hours earlier.

Two - The ward looked like 'One Flew over the Coo Coos Nest. A place you might not wish on your worst enemy.

Three - Deshon's attitude.

"Don't worry about me. I fine here."

It took us all afternoon to get Deshon out of that place.

We stayed with Deshon's adoptive family in Alabama, until time to set out on the two-hour trek back to the airport. They were delightfully hospitable, offering food and lodging to each of the eight people who had caravanned to the hospital when Deshon was discharged.

I got one of the upstairs bedrooms where I was intent on a two-hour nap. I noticed the vibration when I got out of the shower; coming from somewhere outside the bathroom. I dried of and went into my assigned bedroom. The closet door was rattling back and forth, wildly and loudly, against the tongue in the lock jamb.

Anyone else, in any of a thousand other circumstances, would have torn out of there. And politely, or maybe not so politely, asked for a different room. I was beaten bloody by now. I didn't even care. The room was a spare, so there was luggage and laundry baskets in there - maybe (it was dark and I was tired). I just shoved something heavy against the door. I had to shove it much harder before the rattling stopped.

Then I lay on the bed. It was vibrating too. The rhythm was immediately familiar. It was the same as the table, at the restaurant, in front of Morgan the other day. I was oblivious. I went straight to sleep.

Early the next morning, Tory and I boarded the first plane, with a sweet four year old...Deshon.

The next two days were even more of a whirlwind. We were shuffled from hospital to hospital. I must have talked to thirty-five people, from orderlies to doctors. I explained, in detail, our history over the last few days. I didn't know what was relevant, so each time I gave all the details I could think of. Why did it seem to me that some of those people should have given the case background to the next person, before they walked up to us and asked?

"So - what's going on?"

After two days of:

"So - what's going on?"

I was fit to be put in a straight-jacket myself. We were past the hard part. Me and Tory made it down south and came back with Deshon. But as Deshon's condition worsened, strains and divisions showed up in our camp. At one point, I remember hearing the words:

"If depression is the common cold of mental illness, then schizophrenia is the cancer."

That was my lowest point. It really did feel like a life sentence. Deshon had gone from a successful college student, to someone who needed a lifetime of close and painful supervision. I had gone through all those often quoted stages of grief, in just a few days. Prayer was surely in order. I reached out for help in that regard.

We prayed for Deshon. I prayed at Deshon. It wasn't until I prayed *with* Deshon, that the tide began to turn. But, short of a miraculous recovery, how would the family continue to function? I visited Deshon every day, but there were many other considerations.

The hospital continued to put a strain on a financial position that had already been made difficult by my job situation, and more precarious because of the emergency travel. We were coming apart at the seams. If God didn't intervene soon, we'd be overwhelmed.

But God always comes through. And it's always just in time. When faith wears thin, worry takes over and grinds you, like a pencil in a pencil sharpener. More than once, during all this, I said out loud:
"I can't go another day."

God always meets me at that last day. It's the day before the last day that gets me. That day when I feel my fingertips slipping from the ledge. I've heard some say:
"Well just let go and God will catch you."

Let go of what? What's left to let go of, when there's no more hope. Let go of faith? In the last minutes of the last day, there is no faith. There's only now, and the last few seconds that pass painlessly, before the crash. It doesn't take any strength at all. It just happens. That's where God meets me - in between the faiths.

Deshon is at home convalescing, after two weeks in the asylum, and just might be going back to school in a few days. God stepped in with another miracle. I'd gone so far as to think, *Deshon is possessed.* Then I backed off to, *Deshon might be possessed.*

Now I think not - but I don't know. Deshon stuck to a couple of truths throughout the whole ordeal. Something horrible had happened at school. And:

"I died that day in Alabama."

What's left is the fruit of the seeds of division. It grows with a rotting stench, and smells of irreconcilable differences. You never know what straw will break the camel's back, and send everyone fleeing into 'every man for himself' mode.

It's been a few days since I had that dream; the one I had just woken up from when I started writing. I slept the next night, without incident. The nights after that were also uneventful. But that dream still haunts me. I guess it stemmed from visiting Deshon, every night on the psyche ward, at the same time I was giving characterization to a fictional demon.

Some underlying psychosis of my own, combined the two waking pastimes into a horrible dream where I struggled to keep from falling into the pit. Rather, it was more like a funnel; with a big end, and a small end. The big end led to insanity, and it was by far the easier path to go down. I struggled to reach out toward the smaller end, on the side of sanity, but it was too hard.

I grappled with the covers, trying to grab onto Amari, who was lying next to me as I dreamed. I tried calling out, but I wasn't sure which voice Amari would hear. Would it be mine, or would it be the voice of the demon I was writing about. I heard both.

I almost lost myself. I almost fell in. Amari finally responded, and reached over and woke me up. I was on the sane side of the funnel but just barely. The other side is easier. There's no responsibility over there. And nothing left to lose.

Deshon's delusional state was one of grandeur. In mine, I wasn't even human. I can still hear the voice that was trying to call out to my love. If my love had heard it - my love would be gone. Me too - maybe. Or maybe I died that day in the cage.

Maybe I Died: The End

Maybe I died - Author's note: Did you even notice that there were no personal pronouns in the story? You decided the gender of all the characters, yourself.

www.ingramcontent.com/pod-product-compliance
Lightning Source LLC
Chambersburg PA
CBHW060114260626
47160CB00005B/1883